P9-CLQ-412

This place you

return to is home

Also by Kirsty Gunn

Rain
The Keepsake

This place you return to is home

KIRSTY GUNN

Atlantic Monthly Press
New York

The following stories have been published previously: 'The Swimming Pool' and 'Grass, leaves,' in *First Fictions* (Faber & Faber, London, 1992); 'Visitor,' in *Borderlines* (Serpent's Tail, London, 1993); 'Jesus, I know that guy,' in *Slow Dancer Magazine* (Summer 1993); 'Tinsel Bright,' in *A Junky's Christmas* (Serpent's Tail, London, 1994).

First published in Great Britain by Granta Books 1999
Printed in the United States of America

FIRST AMERICAN EDITION

Library of Congress Cataloging-in-Publication Data
Gunn, Kirsty.
This place you return to is home / Kirsty Gunn.
p. cm.
ISBN 0-87113-741-0
1. United States—Social life and customs—20th century —Fiction.
2. Home—United States—Fiction. I. Title.
PS3557.U4864T47 1998
813'.54—dc21 98-39767

Atlantic Monthly Press
841 Broadway
New York, NY 10003

99 00 01 02 10 9 8 7 6 5 4 3 2 1

K. E. S. Gunn 1896–1988

Contents

Not that much to go on

It was a part of the country you forgot about until you were back in the middle of it. Then, thirty miles past the turn-off, how the familiar shape of the land took hold. There were the low yellow hills, rumpled like old carpets, rising up on either side of the car and falling back into paddocks, hillocks. Their worn sides were threadbare, showing grey earth through the thin grass, and not soft to lie on. In places, rocks jutted out like boards, or bone.

Even though you could drive for hours, the woman thought, on bland roads, you would come back to this. For miles the scenery outside the car window had been flat and clean as wallpaper but now there was this cut in the hills, dry shingle track. Deeper and deeper into the interior it followed the knuckled line of the land. There was no space for turning. People who took this route didn't change their minds that way: they left, or they came back. For them, travelling only in one direction was a law of nature – and as she drove further inland the woman felt the tightness of her own compass heart. There was no going back for her either. This was where she belonged. She remembered now.

Since leaving the city this morning and travelling north, what had started as a journey had become her return. Time had changed. The dawn lifting over the city felt like it belonged to another day, and the long highway that led from it. All she knew were these hills, the high flat plain beyond them, the past and future trammelled together by this thin road. She shifted into a lower gear as she felt the car pull back against the incline of the next few yards ahead. All her minutes were here, with the stick, the clutch, all her hours. For a second the motor failed to catch and stalled, whirring, before the gear engaged and the weight of the car's body was forced onwards again, upwards. Slowly, mile by mile, the land gained height. Chips from the road sprang up and hit the windscreen, stones jagged under the chassis. For some time it seemed she was making no progress but still the woman pushed the car further up against the incline, the sides of the hills pressing in, steeper and steeper the road, higher and higher until suddenly the land fell away and the blue sky was everywhere around her. No one would ever find her here. Even from the high saddle there was no sign of the way she'd come, no path, no road, only the bent backs of the hills repeating themselves, over and over, on one side of the road all the way to the western mountains, on the other to the sea.

Now for the woman it was as if she had never been away. The house in the suburbs belonged to someone else, its lawn clipped close as felt. She remembered how grey the lawn had been in the early morning, and moist, her footsteps marked upon it. The woman who had left the house had not used the path. She had closed the front door and walked towards the car; left the racks of tightly-fitted clothes behind her, and the baking pans and tins that gleamed – perhaps some other pretty bride could get the use. Let her go through the cupboards. Let her finger the linen, try on shoes and fancy underwear, use the creams. The one who'd left these things would never want them back. She'd driven through the whole day to get from grey dawn to this blue and yellow afternoon.

She stopped the car, for a minute, to see. All around her the land lay vivid in the light. Although it was late in the day she was too far in high country now for there to be any shadows. Sun streaked the hills and the mountains in the distance were sharp and dark as if they'd been clipped from tin. How far there? What road could take you? As a girl she had always imagined herself walking around those mountain forests, iced with snow and frost – if only the road she knew could take her there, if only, she had thought then, there could be that choice. Now she realized the mountains were no more a fairy tale than any other place. The frost glittering in pieces, the bright frozen leaves – these were brilliants she'd already worn. The snow her white dress, the cold sheets spread across the bed, and the window with the moon in it a pane of ice. The future was simply a set of parts you didn't yet possess. You struggled to lay claim, and the minute you had one you had the rest. Not so the past. That was already deep in: it was this place, earth and sky, these creased hills. It was the few sheep picking at grass along the side of the road for comfort. The woman wound down the window to smell the tang of their wool in the cold air. The past, from now on, was where she always wanted to be.

There wasn't much further to go. She started the engine again, pressing down a little harder on the accelerator. Now that the slow ascent was behind her what was left of the journey would be easy. She increased her speed as the road along the tops lengthened in front of her, wider than before and level. As she drove further west, sun filled the car. It played about the woman's hands resting on the wheel and fell in a bright ribbon across the back seat where her babies were sleeping. In the rear-view mirror she saw them, the girls with their brother carefully between them.

'Good children.' Silently their mother mouthed the words, practising.

'You've been very, very good.'

After all this time they still felt so new. Eleven years had passed since the eldest had been born, and yet even now she felt the longing to rouse them, feel the weight of their bodies in her arms. Was that how it was for a mother? To need to bear your babies for your proof? She wanted so much to keep them to herself, the girls, solemn and dark as strangers, and the tiny boy with quiet watching eyes. Maybe, from now on, the woman hoped, the chance would be there to hold them, be that close.

'Good children,' she practised again.

By taking them back with her, perhaps they would become part of her memory, and not loosen from her mind.

'You're my own children.'

Stay.

They were all she wanted to keep. The rest were trappings. Like the city shoes that had crippled her feet and left prints in the soft grass, her other possessions had made her false and cruel. The fitted band of diamonds said it: *Liar.* If she could wrench it from her finger she would, for days she'd been trying to remove it, soap and water, oil, but all lubricants had failed and the thing remained embedded, as if, like a husband, she was not supposed ever to let it go. The only way to get rid of it now was to cut. Clip the band, throw the bright broken bit to the air and let some bird take it for a nest. Have nothing left. From now on she wanted only the memories of her mother's soft cotton dresses, the smell of them washed in soap and pegged outside on the line to dry. She would have only bare feet, bare hands and her own eyes for brightness. It was a mother's house she wanted for her babies, not a husband's. A familiar place. There would be thin curtains billowing at the window in the morning sunshine, the paper blind tapping on the glass in a slight breeze and the print of the window frame upon it each time it touched. There would be summer and autumn and winter and spring, endless blue days, some with frost and others with the hot smell of grass in them and hay, but apart from that all the days the same and wide as air with nothing in them.

As she drove she felt more and more these promises of her destination. Her hands on the wheel felt them, and her keen eyes trained on distance. There would be the final curve of the road, the dip in the land . . . In her mind she was already there. Now she was driving up the main street, passing Farm Supplies, and the milk bar where the kids hung around outside, sipping cokes and smoking. How quiet it was, and the little shops seemed closed. On the shadowy side of the street the thin iron colonnades outside Dalgety's stood in a row, t[illegible] pretty glass roof broken in bits, and a brittle wind coursing through it. In the store windows were the swathes of patterned cloth she remembered, the tilted mannequin dressed in a cocktail gown, the twisted metal stand of hats. She tried to look inside for more but it was dark. In her mind she crossed the street, but though it was sunny and warm enough to sit on the bench outside the post office, there was nobody there. The cabinet outside had a notice pinned inside it advertising postal rates for a Christmas long since passed.
'Your last chance for surface parcels.'
'Don't be late with your greetings.'
Next door, Ballard's Fruit had the blind pulled down, and in the window of Jim Reed's the colouring books and boxes of toys were faded and dusty. A bumble-bee dozed on a pack of cards, a dead fly rested in the pink lacy lap of a plastic baby doll.

Everything was exactly as she remembered it. No people in the street, empty shops, nothing in the world to buy. Though to a visitor the town may have seemed shocked timeless by an unexpected death, for the woman it was as if her return had been arranged. The poor toys and favours were not gaudies for a grave but mementoes. As she dreamed, it seemed even the thin wind in the street was an echo, her own lovely refrain.

All gone.

All gone.

The empty bottle rolling along the footpath, the ruffle of paper rubbish in the gutter.

All gone.

The road had opened out by now, the narrow track given way to a band of tarmac that was smooth and long. A low bank of grass grew on either side with fence posts behind, fixed up with wire. She knew she was getting closer then. Though the paddocks were empty and the wood on the fence posts so worked and softened with moss one quick push could bring the whole line down, even so they meant some farmer had put them there. He would be back. Soon, she would see a house. Then another. Then she'd feel the dip in the land and the turn as the road began curving up into town.

'Mummy.'

In the back seat, one of the children shifted in sleep.

The woman pressed down on the accelerator. She knew this

part of the plain. She recognized the squeak of the wire on the posts. As a girl, she'd climbed over them: one foot on the base wire, the other on the top. There was the brief blunt cut of the wire printed into her bare soles then she swung one leg over and jumped down the other side. The grass felt thick and soft.

'Mummy.'

She knew exactly where she was. There were the clumps of toi-toi up ahead, gathered together in clumps along the banks where the land scooped out in a shallow bowl.

'Mummy, please.'

'Shhh.'

Without turning her head she put her fingers to her lips and whispered, 'Look.' She pointed out the window. 'They all belong to me.'

Along the bank the toi-toi had gathered, hundreds of them, to welcome her. They waved their soft braided heads, pale blond like the hair of babies, each seeded strand combed by the thin breeze. When she had been a child she'd played with them, straddled their cane stems, ridden them like horses through the hills. She'd plaited the blond manes, kissed their heads.

There now, easy.

Even now she could hear them whinny and snort as they gathered around her, her tall palominos.

Good girl, easy.

How young she'd been. She'd worn slip dresses cut from her

mother's own, her arms and legs had been left open to the air.

Easy, girl.

Outside the window of her car the pale horses surrounded her, all their blond heads nodding, dipping in the breeze. She could play with them now.

In the rear-view mirror her eyes, for a second, caught the eyes of a child who had woken. Was she the same one who had been calling to her? Again the woman had the shock of strangeness, like fear. Who was she? Then she remembered, the present came back at her. She remembered what to do.

'Shhh.'

Again she put her fingers to her lips, whispered so softly it was like breath.

'We're nearly there, I'll wake you when we stop. Sleep now. Don't disturb the others.'

It must be the second one who had woken. Always it was the younger girl who asked questions. In the morning it had been the same.

'But where are we going? How long will it take?'

Born two years after her sister it was as if she had to know why all the time, to be given the comfort of information to make up for being second in line, the one who comes after the procession and picks up, picks up.

'Will we like it? Will there be a school there?'

Always questions, so many words.

'But why are we going today? Why now? What made you decide?'

They had stood outside the house in the dawn. Mist rose from the pale grey of the footpath.

'Where will we live? Will we have a house of our own?'

Although the daughter had been whispering, the mother heard the loudness of accusation in her words. Anyone might hear; across the grey lawn, inside the house a husband, sleeping, might hear the questions through his dreams.

'Why are we leaving so early, Mummy? Why isn't Daddy coming too?'

The light outside the car window had blanched now, shadows made troughs in the back hills, the sun that had played about the woman's hands had gone. Up ahead the road curved, no signpost to mark it, no map. She had come this far. With all the questions in the world, no one would ever guess she had brought her children here.

Finally it had been the older girl who had managed to silence the other. When the last bag was stacked in the boot, the last cardboard box squashed into the space on the back shelf, she ran into the house and came out carrying the baby. Without a word she put him, bundled in a blanket, into her sister's arms. That was when the mother and the daughters knew that the words were finished between them. The mother had opened the car door and the girls climbed in, took the baby between them. She'd closed the door after them, then she herself slid into the driver's seat and turned the key in the ignition. Before it was properly light she had pressed down the clutch and eased the gears through first, second, down the driveway. In third she had moved the car, soundlessly it seemed, through the sleeping suburban streets. In fourth she had left the city. Seventy miles an hour on the main roads to put the distance down, fifty from the turn-off, dropping down when the surface was bad. Back out along the high country she'd made an easy sixty. There was so much time to lose in the miles she left behind.

'You can do anything with your life,' that's what everyone had always told her.

Alright, so she would do it now. After all the years, after all the strange city women with their powdered scented cheeks, their whisperings in her ear, 'You're so very, very young.'

After falling in love, and marriage, and the tightness of the ring . . . Here, amongst her familiar hills, with the dark coming up behind, she knew what to do.

'Are we going where you lived with your mother? Will we like it there?'

That morning she had pressed her cold face up against her second daughter's cold face.

'Please, please,' she'd whispered. 'No more questions now.'

Tonight they would be back there, that was all. It was simple. Though the woman driving the car had buried her mother years ago the house she had grown up in would be there and they could claim it; they would open the door. Though it would be night when they arrived they would be comforted by the surround of its walls, the planes of window and door. One by one they would walk into unoccupied rooms, feel the shape of the house form around them. Room by room, in the dark, they would feel it. The woman driving the car had this knowledge in herself; fate. Home.

Not that much to go on: 2

The waxed floor of the library squeaked when she walked on it. And there was the smell of wax and polish, she remembered that from when she'd been here before. The high windows were open to the blue sky and sunlight filled the newly-dusted room, fell across the long wooden shelves of books. The girl did not know of a place that was more clean, more light and high inside. Sometimes the librarians had a glass vase of flowers on the desk where they stamped her books, tall stems of thick pink stocks, or bundles of daisies, and it was as if even the water they stood in was the clearest you could scoop into a jar. As if the million tiny bubbles on the bunched green stems were beaded there, each clear water droplet intricately suspended. As if the air and the water and the glass were cut clean out of the light.

'Hello Mary Susan. It's nice to see you again.'
The librarian looked up at her when she came in the door.
'Is your little sister not with you this time?'
The girl shook her head. The librarians were so beautiful she found it hard to talk to them. Only when she was taking out a book, or asking where she might find a particular section in the library. Only when she had a proper library question to ask could she look full into the face of the beautiful ladies, let her eyes touch.
'Excuse me,' she could say then, and not feel so shy. 'Where can I find the books for cooking? For learning to make tiny clothes for dolls?'

And when the librarians kindly helped her, taking her by the hand sometimes, to find the proper shelf, it gave her confidence to talk to them a little. It was because they asked her about books, and she found those sorts of questions easier to answer than the others.

'How do you like living in the country?'

That was one question.

Or, 'Did mother make you that pretty dress?'

Or, 'Have you met any of the other schoolchildren now that term has begun?'

It was still summer, but in the library it did feel as though a new term had begun. Already the children from the nearby school had made twig and branch arrangements for autumn. They had brought them to the library one day last week, as Mary Susan was walking away she saw them arrive. There were about ten boys and girls, probably most of the school because here it was the country and not like the city school where she'd been before with lots and lots of children in the class. She had watched them, from around the back of the library, coming in the front door holding tall bare branches that they'd stuck with paper leaves coloured red and yellow and bright orange, even though nobody had ever seen a really bright orange leaf, or a red, they were mostly brown or dark green in real life. Still, the branch arrangements were very beautiful and Mary Susan wished she could have made one. She would have liked to kneel on a bare floor with the other children and cut out leaf shapes and colour them. From her hiding place she watched them take the branches into the library, and when they were inside, she came around and peeped in the window. The librarians were helping them tie the branches up onto the walls as decoration and make a display of special autumn books on the table beneath. They covered the table with a green cloth to look like a hill, and scattered more paper leaves on it, and on the books.

Mary Susan went back and told her sister Elisabeth about the whole idea and that night they made an autumn display of their own in the bedroom they shared in the new house.
'I'll be the librarian helping you choose an autumn book,' Mary Susan said to Elisabeth.
'You can be one of the children from school, and you're my favourite so I help you the most.'

The librarians were beautiful, of course Mary Susan wanted to be one of them. They wore pink smocks, ironed like sheets of fresh paper, over their ordinary clothes, and special white gloves sometimes, when they had something particular to do with new books, like cover them with plastic, or stick in the white returns slip, with its little matching card pocket. This way, with white gloves on, they could use glue without staining their fingers. They could turn brand new pages without making a single mark.

★

There was one young librarian, who Mary Susan wanted to be most, and an older one with pale grey hair shiny like silver. They were both tall women. They wore sandals and their faces were clean. Only the young librarian wore pale pink lipstick, and her fingernails, when Mary Susan saw her turn to the back of a book to stamp the return date, were also pink and glossy. This could have been polish, Mary Susan knew, like her mother used to wear when they lived in the city, or it could have been that the young librarian had simply wiped her nails with oil at night and rubbed them with a cloth until they gleamed. Either way, she didn't mind. The librarian was beautiful.

Mary Susan watched the librarian's hands move daintily among the books she had chosen, checking each one had no old return date in it, or that the plastic cover was neat. Then she arranged them in a lovely stack of four on the library counter.

'Most of the other children can only take out three books at a time,' she had told Mary Susan last time. 'But from now on I'm going to let you take four. Because I know how much you love to read and I know how careful you are with the books at home.'

In the background, through the light warm air, classical music played. The silvery notes from flutes and thin violin strings. Like everything else in the library it was light and clear and pure. Like a clear running stream. Like a glass of cold water. Carefully Mary Susan picked up her pile of books. She felt very careful.

The librarian was right, she and Elisabeth did read a lot of books. Sometimes they went to the library every day during the week, when they were the only people there, or every other day, but they always read all their books in between. It was a queer time. Not at school but the days still hot and full of blue sky so it felt like summer holidays anyway. They could read as many books as they wanted and make believe they were only on holiday in the country. Any day their mother might wake them up early in the morning and they would pack their bags and drive back to the city. They would go back to their own house where their father lived and they would go back to their old school. And everything would be the same as before.

The truth was, and Mary Susan knew this in the part of her heart that felt like a sharp corner, that they wouldn't be going home. The strange empty house where they lived now, where their mother had lived when she was a little girl, that was where they had to stay. On a street that only had three other houses in it, with paddocks all around and fields of silky green turning yellow in the late afternoon sun, and in the distance hills, far trees. Her mother kept saying this part of the country was their real home and Mary Susan's cornered heart felt the queerness of it, being so far away. And every day, another hot day, and no school, only books to read in a dark room sitting with Elisabeth on the sofa, their legs touching for comfort, as they read, because their mother wasn't there again. She'd taken the baby that morning and walked out across the paddocks in bare feet, not telling them where she was going.

So the girls kept the library routine. They put their books in two piles by the sofa at their feet, one pile of read and one of unread books, and they swapped them over when they were done. That was the plan. Only think about reading. Only think about getting to the end of each story. At the window of the sitting room the sky showed blue and quiet as if nothing had happened, and Mary Susan sometimes looked up from reading, at the square of sky, and for a minute she thought she was looking out of her bedroom window back at home, and that she was still there, reading a book there.

Then she remembered where she was. She left her place on the sofa to walk across the floor, down the hall and out the front door and the strangeness of the house formed fully around her again. All the rooms were nearly empty, the air resting on a bed, at a dusty window, waiting. Here was the house where her grandmother had died, her mother's mother and she'd never known her. Now there was little of her left. There was nothing in the drawers or cupboards, only the few things their mother had packed, left to hang loosely in the wardrobes. There was no food in the funny old-fashioned Frigidaire that they hadn't put there themselves, or in the kitchen cupboards that were so old. They were strange, the wooden surrounds painted red and yellow and green, with bone handles and wire on the fronts so Mary Susan could see inside them as if they were birdcages, or traps for small animals. Outside the house, when she opened the front door, the strangeness bloomed and grew. There was so much air. Everywhere, the smell of dried grass, of animals grazing, the deep warm smell of sunshine settled into the earth, and sometimes, after rain, a fresh sweetness that came from the garden. Their mother said their grandmother had been such a gardener that she had planted some things especially for the day she knew they would come and live here. Sweet peas growing on the back wall for the girls, strawberries for the baby, and a trimmed rose tree for her, growing right outside her old bedroom window.

'She knew we would come back,' Mary Susan's mother told her. 'She prepared things for us, so that we would have her garden to look after when she was gone. That you girls would grow up here in sweet air. We don't have to worry about anything any more.'

This was how their mother spoke to the girls in the evening, when it was time for them to go to sleep in the big double bed in their grandmother's old room. She looked outside to the garden as she spoke, and further away, past the hedge, to

the far fields and the trees. The sound of birds came through the half-opened window, and the room was filled with warmth and the scent of violets and last light.
'You will get used to it here.' Her mother tucked them in. 'You'll see, it's very special.'

As she left the darkening room, tiptoeing because the baby in the other bed was already asleep, Mary Susan saw her mother had no shoes on. That meant she was going out again, even at night, while they were sleeping. Mary Susan looked over at Elisabeth, hoping she hadn't seen, but Elisabeth was already soothed into sleep by her mother's gentle dreamy words. If she woke in the night Mary Susan would have to comfort her. She would have to lie. She would say that their mother was asleep in the dark house, even though really she was outside somewhere, running across the paddocks in bare feet. Not even the baby in her arms to remind her of her real life, of her children, Mary Susan thought, of her husband.

When she got up in the morning it was as if nothing had happened. Her mother was sitting in the kitchen smoking a cigarette, like she'd been sitting there every morning since they'd come up here. The breakfast things were all laid out.
'Just like you asked me,' her mother said.
Mary Susan sat down and reached for a piece of toast, the butter, the jam.
'Just like you asked, strawberry jam.' Her mother drew on her

cigarette, then put back her head and let the air come out of her mouth in a soft grey cloud. She seemed so careless, as if all her thoughts were light and soft as grey smoke. She was smiling. She inhaled again then ground out what was left of the cigarette in the ashtray. 'Don't worry, darling. No horrid smoking while you're having your special breakfast.'

Mary Susan didn't say the toast was cold. Who knew when her mother had made it? How long she had been sitting out in the sunny kitchen, with all her make-up on. She looked down at her mother's feet. Stains of wet earth were on them.

'What are you going to do today, sweetheart?'
Her mother suddenly started fiddling with the pack of cigarettes. 'Any special plans?'
She tapped the pack on the table in a little rhythm, rat-a-tat, rat-a-tat.
'Because if you don't mind I might just pop out for a bit, sometime, I don't know when. You're such a good girl, could you look after things here for me? Maybe pick up some shopping, give Baby his tea?'
Mary Susan just nodded. She would never in the world ask why. Ask why her mother did any of the things, where she had gone last night, or where she went every day. She carefully chewed her toast and then swallowed. Even though it was dry the jam was sticky and she could eat another piece.

Her mother tried so hard for her so she would never ask.
'I love you Mummy,' Mary Susan said instead.

That day was a library day. The sisters experimented with taking their own sandals off and walking up to the village in bare feet. The heat of the sun had fired the black tarmac of the road like a pan so they had to keep stepping onto the thick grass clumps that grew in the gutter to cool off. Already the skin on their soles was burnt, blackened with cooked dirt.
'This is what Mummy does,' said Elisabeth, as they walked, pointing her feet in a dainty way, the way their mother made her pretty little dancer's steps.
'And this.' Mary Susan had rolled up a leaf for a cigarette, and she puffed it, balancing the baby on her hip as she'd seen her mother do.
'*Hey, hey. La di la,*' sang Elisabeth, making her lips kiss in the air like their mother did when she sang her tuneless made-up songs.
'*Hey, hey*.' Mary Susan joined in. 'Mummy does this too,' she said, letting her hair fall over one eye. She smoked her leaf cigarette.
'I know,' said Elisabeth, putting her head on one side so her hair fell in the same way. 'And this.' She flicked it back by tossing her head. 'Like this.' She started repeating the gesture over and over, flicking her head forward then back, forward and back. 'Like this, like this, like this,' and Mary Susan wanted to do it too, she wanted to put down the baby and let

her hair flick and fall and move. Then Elisabeth stopped. She looked up.
'What do you think Mummy is doing now?'
Suddenly Mary Susan felt wrong. What a silly thing to do. She brushed her silly hair off her face.
'I think it must be a surprise,' she said, but slowly, and she felt the corner of her heart as she spoke. 'Like coming here was a surprise. And not having to go to school.'

Anyway, today they had money. Their mother had given it to them for the shopping but there was enough left over for them to have lunch at the milk bar tearooms if they wanted, that was like a surprise. They could choose proper ice creams, different pastel flavours put together in a pretty glass dish with cream. Or they could have a milk shake and cakes with pink icing and a ham sandwich. Mary Susan had a bottle in her shoulder bag for Baby's lunch. She could ask the lady at the milk bar to warm it, her mother had said, if, for example, they wanted to stay out all day.
'I think we would like to,' Mary Susan had said, when her mother suggested it at breakfast.
'I think it would be fun,' her mother replied. 'Why not?'

So really, it *was* like a surprise day now. Not a lie at all. They were having an adventure. Going to the library first to take back their books and get out some others. Then walking along to the tearooms on the high street to choose the things

for lunch. They would sit there at the special tables in the back, away from the front of the shop, she and Elisabeth with their baby, just like grown-ups.
How are you, Mrs Smith?
Very well. How are you, Mrs Jones?
Very well, thank you.
And how is your lovely baby?

So it could be the sort of day that was just like a real school holiday. Elisabeth even said she had all the pocket money Daddy had given her and she was going to spend it at the toyshop.
'Might you buy something we can share?' Mary Susan asked.
'I'm going to buy something for all of us,' said Elisabeth. 'You and me and Mummy, and the baby, and Daddy too. A kind of toy we can all use.'

It didn't take long to walk up to the village. Even with Mary Susan holding the heavy baby, and with the shoulder bag bumping down against her leg. Even with walking barefoot on the hot road where there were stones or on the thick grass that had prickles. It could never take too long to walk there. It was such a small place where their mother had brought them. One street with some shops, some houses near the street, a playground that only had a set of swings and a slide. Nothing was far away from anything else. Even the library on the other side of town from the shops was only round the corner of the high street, up the hill a little way towards the school. Even if Mary Susan wanted to take as much time as she could walking to the library, she couldn't use up much of the day. Even if she stopped many times on the way to rearrange the weight of a bag on her shoulder, or a baby. Even if she sat down at every lamp-post to pick the prickles one by one from her feet.

The librarians were pleased to see them when they arrived. It was because of the baby. They were pleased to see him.
'Ah! There he is at last, the little darling.'
The older librarian came straight out from behind the counter and was upon the girls in a second.
'May I have him for a bit?'
She leaned down and unwrapped him from Mary Susan, took him up for herself, kissing him, then she held him up for the other librarian to see.
'Look at him! What a little darling!'

The young librarian came over then, and they both stood close together in a tiny little group, holding Baby and kissing him, letting him dribble down their clean pink smocks.
'He's adorable. I'm so glad you've let us meet him at last. What responsible girls to be allowed to bring him here on your own.'
Mary Susan stepped back.
The young librarian's voice was not whispering and pretty like

before. The older one came forward to give the baby back to Mary Susan and her mouth opened up wide, coming right up to Mary Susan as if she wanted to press the words onto her face. 'Mother must know she can really rely on you.'

Now she leaned even closer to Mary Susan.

'I expect you girls are a great help around the house. Is that right? Are you both a great help to your mother?'

Mary Susan felt her face get hot. Now that she had Baby again she could pretend to bury her face in his muslin cloths, as if she was kissing him or peering closely at him, but really it was because she couldn't answer that question.

'Is that right, dear?' the librarians were saying, but she couldn't answer any of the questions.

'What do you think?'

Instead Elisabeth replied. She was never supposed to do that.

'Don't forget our Daddy,' she said. 'We help him too. He's the one that makes us a real family, not Mummy. It's Daddy we need. Soon he'll come and live with us here, or take us back to the city to our own home. Baby is his, really. He loves him most. He'll have to come looking for him soon.'

'Shhh.'

Mary Susan tried to stop the flow of words but Elisabeth's voice went on and on in the empty calm room of the library. On and on, talking to strangers. She was never supposed to do that. Talking all the secrets out loud into the air.

'We're only a part of a family now, but it will all fix up soon,' she was saying. 'I'm buying a toy, later, that will help it fix. And Mummy will take us home again.'

Mary Susan turned, still holding the baby, and started walking away so that Elisabeth would follow. She would have to follow, she would have to turn and follow and not listen to any more questions. Surely she would have to stop talking now. But as Mary Susan walked all she could hear was Elisabeth's voice getting louder and louder, like crying, worse than before. She turned around to pull her away then stopped, shocked still with fright at what she saw. Elisabeth was standing right beside the older librarian and she was reaching for her arm and touching it, pressing up close to her as if she wanted to be picked up. Then Mary Susan saw the librarian take her hand, and fold Elisabeth into her.

'I know Mummy is going to take us home,' Elisabeth was saying, and now she was crying. 'And then we'll go back to our real house, and our real school. We won't need to go to this library, or have to stay on our own all day.'

Mary Susan saw the older librarian give the other one a quick look, like a little arrow, and they both knew the message of the arrow. Still she couldn't move. The younger librarian leaned down towards Elisabeth and instead of smiling she had a worried, poisoned look on her face. She was much, much too close. 'What did you say, sweetie?' she said. 'Do you mean Mummy leaves you all alone during the day?'

Her voice was quiet. Everything in the library was quiet. The librarian's breath was on Elisabeth's face. Her hair was touching. She wasn't even a member of the family and she was acting like she knew them, like she could come up close to Elisabeth in that way with her questions. Again Mary Susan felt the corner of her heart turn in on her. It turned towards her stomach so that she felt sick and black and with no breath in her.

'What did you say, darling?' the librarian was saying with her pale pink lips. 'About Mummy?'

Mary Susan couldn't bear it, the closeness of her lips. She was still beautiful, the librarians would always be beautiful, but now the special feeling she'd had for them was spoiled. There were too many questions. Nobody should have asked any questions, like Mary Susan didn't ask them, to stay safe. Nobody should ask anything about their family, or what they did. They were on their own and they looked after themselves, that's what their mother had said. It was destiny, it was nobody's business. Nobody's business what they did, and why they came to the country and how long they stayed.

'One day you will go to school here and it will all work out fine,' her mother had said, but that was a lie. It was best not to ask a question at all if you only got a lie. Best to remember what her mother had said in the car, it seemed a long time ago, when they were coming to this place.

'Please. No more questions now.'

*

Mary Susan went over to Elisabeth and took her by the arm.
'Come on.'
She pulled her harder, away from the librarian who was stroking her.
'Come on. We have to leave.'
Her head was down as she spoke, so she wouldn't have to see the librarian full in the face, and she suddenly knew what she could say.
'Elisabeth, you know we're not wearing any shoes. Every person in a library must wear shoes.'
She pulled Elisabeth's arm a little more and the librarian let go of her hand. Elisabeth was still sobbing, but quietly now.
'We don't mind if she doesn't want to wear shoes,' the librarian said.
'Well, I do mind,' said Mary Susan, right back at her.

They left the library then and everywhere she looked were dirty marks on the wax floor. There were black marks all around the door, where she and Elisabeth had come in, black marks trodden right into the library, all over the polished floor the black dirty footprints they had made.
'Please come back and see us again soon,' called the librarians after them, but they didn't turn around. Everything was spoiled now. The floor marked, stains of Elisabeth's tears on the librarian's smock, dribbled bits from the baby. They couldn't go back there.

*

'Come on. Hurry.'

Mary Susan nearly ran out the door, down the library path past the tall blue tree that grew on the lawn outside.

'Come on.'

Behind them they could just hear the high silvery sounds of the library music coming out in waves through the open window. Then everything was quiet. Not even the baby cried.

They wouldn't go to the toyshop now, or for the special lunch to choose cakes in the window like ladies. Instead Mary Susan just pulled Elisabeth and she came easily behind her. Her tears had dried but her face looked dirty and blotched.

'My feet hurt.'

Mary Susan looked down and saw that Elisabeth's feet were like hers, marked with mud, and also crusted with bits of dirt from running in the open with no shoes. They never used to be like that. In the city they would wear pretty sandals if it was hot, or thin leather shoes with white socks.

'Come on.'

She tugged Elisabeth again and her cornered heart twisted, set. It was all changed. It wouldn't be the same again. Mary Susan knew from now on it would always be dirty feet, from being outdoors alone. Just like their mother's feet had been that morning, with no protection, not clean.

The swimming pool

You could hear the kids yelling in the pool.

Through the hot air, you could hear them, the sound of them playing in that blue swimming pool water. They'd be tossing up water and throwing it around so it made silvery strings against the dark blue sky. They sounded far away, those kids, but they were only up the road, in the park where the pool was. They were like a crowd cheering, happy for something.

And the silvery strings, your arms tossing up the bright water, a million glittery bits. Remember how it felt?

We weren't doing anything much, just sitting on the front steps, and Billy was burning up ants with a magnifying glass.
'Zap!'
It's not cruel. The ants don't know it's happening because it's instant death. They simply feel a heat on their heads, like the sun only hotter, then – pop!
'Incineration!'
Kitty says it's quite humane, the speed of it. 'It's probably the best way to die.'
Is humane the same as human?
'There's no pain, you see,' says Kitty. 'They don't feel a thing.'

I was watching them, those little lines of ants. They were running along the side of a crack, then down into a hole where it was cool and dark. I could imagine them running along their corridors, in and out of their tiny doors, running through their ant rooms. They were so busy they wouldn't be checking up on their friends. There were so many of them, how could they know who was missing?

What happened was that Billy chose one ant and followed him with the magnifying glass, holding it over his head so it cast a wide circle of light around him. It could have been the ant's own little circus ring lit up with floodlights, getting hotter and hotter and –

'Got him!'

Billy had one pile of sugar for bait and another pile of deads. They're so teeny-weeny when they're dead, just a crumb or a bit of dust. Like a fairy's raisin, that's how small.

Billy was counting the pile.

'Twenty,' he said. 'Twenty trillion to go!'

Lots of kids play this game, not only us. And we weren't particularly playing it, it was just a thing to do. It was pretty hot, that day, the concrete on the front steps was baking. I could feel it through my dress, which was my best dress. Queer, to be in best clothes in the middle of the week. Church, when it wasn't a Sunday. I could feel how crammed up my feet were from having to wear shoes and socks. And up the road you could hear all those kids in the pool. Jumping around in the water, sliding around in it like we used to.

*

No one was stopping us swimming, it wasn't a rule. It was just that we . . .

Maybe it was something to do with having the pool so close, that we didn't feel grateful enough for it. Maybe that's why we don't go any more.

It's not that the pool isn't good, you see, because it is. Other kids go to it all the time. From far away even, they come especially, on the train, just to swim in it. You can see them, from my bedroom window, walking up our road. Their towels are rolled into sausages under their arms and their togs mashed inside. Some of the girls have proper beach bags to carry various things: e.g. suntan lotion. Kitty has a bag like that, with a special compartment that zips and with little loops for lip-salve and, I suppose, lipstick.

'Promise you won't tell!'

She's not allowed to wear make-up, Dad says so.

'But I do promise!'

'Swear!'

Another thing I would never tell on is the kids who smoke. Mostly train kids, and they do it in the changing sheds so no one can see and report them. I bet half of them just come to the pool so they can be away from their parents and the girls can wear bikinis and not feel ashamed.

*

So many kids come down our road. They all know each other, that's how they act, like they're all each other's friends and in a group. In the morning the sun makes prints on the footpath and the sky is pale blue and fresh, it reminds me of a flower. Then at evening, when the pool is closed, those kids come back down our road. Golden, from the way the sun is setting, the sun low over the bush, last slivers of it over the edge of the hills.

Then those kids go home, only then. When everyone's tired from the sun and the water. They've got iceblocks and sweets from the swimming pool shop, the coloured packets they leave in the gutter of our road. They drag their feet along the footpath, or play granny steps and walking backwards. They have iceblock fights and some boys flick some girls with their towels – for instance, the girls who walk home with their bikinis on. Or just a towel wrapped around but leaving the top bare.

'Martin Thomas, I'm going to get you.'

'That really hurt.'

'You're in for it!'

You can hear them laughing, those girls aren't really mad. You can hear everything they say from my bedroom window.

'Sally Davies is in lu-u-u-rve!'

And someone whistling at her.

They don't have to be at home at a certain time, those particular kids. They're more teenagers, anyhow. They don't even have to wear shoes, not even jandals. Sometimes, at school, they don't wear shoes. My mother said it was because they were poor.

'If you have an extra piece of fruit at lunchtime, you ought to give it to those poor little train children.' That's what she said then.

But they weren't even little!

'They don't get the opportunities with fruit that you children get.'

Like they were orphans! Or out of some sad book! When we knew the truth which was that they did things like smoke and kiss with tongues.

If my mother had known what they were really like, if we had told her, would she still have said those kind words?

But my brother Billy loved the train kids.

When he used to go to the pool, before he stopped going to the pool, he used to go with this gang who came from six stops away on the train. From those funny houses that were all stuck together and faced the station and didn't even have gardens. My mother didn't know anything that went on between those kids and my brother. But Billy did get up to real live stuff with the Parsons boys. It wasn't just talk.

I never told on him though, I wouldn't have.

'Billy's been jumping over the swimming pool fence and not paying!' – this was a sentence, for instance, that I would never have told my mother. Or, 'Billy's been hanging around with the Parsons boys at the pool and nicking change from the custodian's office.'

I didn't tell on him to my mother because that kind of information would have made her even more sad. When she couldn't bear some particular piece of information, there was this one sentence she used: 'You children are going to make me very ill.'

These were the kinds of thoughts going on that afternoon, sitting on the hot steps. But trying not to think them too, humming some dumb tune.

It was so still with the heat. Like sitting in a painted garden, being on a stage with the bright lights turned way up. Because everyone had been looking at us, all day, because of what had happened. Starting with us having to walk in separately and sit right in the front of the church. Only now no one was looking any more, it was only us, and Billy doing this thing to the ants.

'Whoosh!'

Another ant made a little pop – and died.

'Oh, man.' That's Kitty. Oldest and all the time acting like she's so cool. Like this day for instance, the day that I'm talking about, she was wearing blue eyeshadow. Acting so neat and tidy with her little blue eyelids going flippety-flip. Still, I knew that if I told her that the eyeshadow looked dumb she would have started to cry. Acting so neat and tidy but tears could easily have come bursting out. Just one little word is all it would have taken.

It was that sort of day when any dumb thing could have happened. Like when Billy killed the first ant I laughed so hard I was sick. A combination of the ants and the chocolate people had been shoving at us all day. Why do people only give you fancy chocolates as a sly thing? Why is it always that they only give you chocolates when some bloody old horrible thing happens?

That word bloody.

Swearing too used to make my mother sad. Bloody this, bloody that. It was another bad habit Billy caught from the Parsons kids. Once, in the hospital, he screamed bloody-bloody-bloody all the way down the corridor. Who knows why. Perhaps because those corridors always made you think they were the only things left. Like there was nothing else in your life except walking down those stinking corridors, going for miles and miles down them, until you got to the right door.

Bloody-bloody-bloody.

Like they were the only things, stinking bloody stupid corridors, like hospital was the only thing in our lives. Like it wasn't even summer because there wasn't the feeling of being on holidays. Instead it was always being inside, the same smell, the same stupid sicky green colour on the walls and on the floor and everywhere. The hospital smell and that sicky old colour. Like the kind of puke you might have if you were taking bloody old pills and having some machine –

When Billy got to her room he said 'I bloody hate you' to my mother and she didn't even tell him off. She just let him put his head on her lap, even though we weren't really supposed to touch her, just put his head on her lap and she patted his hair.

That's the sort of thing I meant before about not knowing what could happen next.

Like how weird it was that even though it was summer we hadn't been going up to the pool any more. All those kids were up there yelling, you could hear them having fun. Ducking each other and dive-bombing off the high dive – although I'm frightened of doing that – still a lot of kids think it's fun. Hitting off the high dive – wham! Straight onto the blue water.

I did it once. That minute, that tiny second when you hit the water flat on, you lose your breath. All the air flattens out of you – like going flat out on concrete. Then the next second you're sliding through, sliding and sinking slowly to the bottom of the pool. You touch the bottom, you bounce once there gently like an astronaut. And you feel the bottom of the pool against the soles of your feet and that's queer – but not queer, because you're the same person, aren't you? Just in another place that's all, you've still got the same body there. You look around, in that blue time, in that deep place. You look around with the same eyes, at the milky chlorine blue, and you have so much time there. Deep in the water with your same body, but everything's different, everything's better.

I'm never coming up again.
I wave my arms, so white and fishy down there, my arms like some old squid, wavering like a beautiful flower, my fingertips could be tentacles, sucking, sucking – soft little noises. There, do you hear them? Under here where it's nice? Those quiet little tentacle sounds? And there too, you hear the beating of your own blood, the air in your own head – it's you, wanting to come back to yourself, wanting to float back up to the top and breathe a mouthful again.

'Once upon a time . . .' You know those stories you have when you're a kid? And your mother makes up the stories and you are always in them? Like, for example, you are the sort of hero who rescues a person when they fall off a cliff. You put their bones into the right sort of bandage so that the wound will heal and not cause so much pain for the injured person.

And you make a stretcher from driftwood and things you find on the beach – a fishing net, say, and an old bit of rope to tie it onto the twigs with. And all this happens near to where the person's body is lying. So you put that sick person on the stretcher and carry it all the way up the cliff yourself, up some narrow little rocky path – once, you nearly fall yourself! But there, you're safe, and you're going across the paddock to . . . Look! A little house in the distance! And you ask if you can use the phone and the people let you, and you call the ambulance, and the ambulance people come and you know what they say. They say, 'You saved that person's life!' You! You saved it! You managed to do that even though that person seemed almost dead and not the person you knew at all. So the story ends happily ever after. Ever, ever, ever.

I used to have a bunch of friends myself. And we used to go swimming together up at the pool. I mean, I went with them to the pool and we had some fun there, making up ideas about how to swim, and doing things based on the Olympic Games.

Thinking, I was thinking there as I sat on the steps that day: I'll bet those same people are up at the pool right now, running around the edge of it and then – tipping over in: Man Overboard! The favourite drowning game. Overboard into where it's pale blue and quiet. So gentle there with your fishy arms. And strings of water like necklaces hanging from you.

You would think the fun feeling of that game was a feeling you could rely on. Wouldn't you think that? But no, because now swimming gives me no pleasure. You can hear the kids there at the pool, the same kids, but even though it's the middle of summer you're not going up there. Even with it being so hot that the dog's stretched out like a rug on the steps, just the little corner of his tongue showing, sleeping like he's never going to wake.

'Zap!' Another one.
Billy's magnifying glass came out of a set that one of the aunts gave him in the morning, after we'd all come back from the church. It was one of those days for presents. Like the fancy chocolates that come in big boxes with ribbons that are so pretty you could use them in your hair. Those fancy presents, and all the dumb flowers.

'Twenty-one and counting.'
My father was inside the dark house, perhaps sleeping. Perhaps listening for the telephone.
'Zap him!' Billy was laughing, then it was quiet again. The quiet shadow of the magnifying glass, casting its eye upon the concrete – the worst kind of sun for ants.

And far away – can you hear it? The noise of the others? Those little voices from miles and miles away, nowhere near you?

*

It's all kid stuff, putting ribbons in your hair. Having people around you like it's supposed to be fun. Kitty's got that blue slick on her eyes and it's the only thing left of the swimming pool she's taking with her.

'We've got to go on.' That's what my father said.

Kitty's got that glinty blue eyeshadow on because she thinks the next best thing to going on is growing up. The colour dribbles down her cheeks, like little bits of the pool. That dumb swimming pool is where all those other kids will be going to for the rest of their lives. You could tell, just by listening to them, they were all there that day.

Grass, leaves

Nan reckons rain. Feels the big, sticky clouds, she says, pumpkin yellow and mean as a man's eye, piling up over the far mountains. In her mind's eye she sees it, the storm. Brewing to pour and the air aching for it. The poor ground's dusty mouth gaping for water.

In the paddocks across the road, cows doze and the sheep pick at stubble grasses. The land behind them goes barren and lost all the way to the sky. It's our view, it's safe. I could dream all day up here with Nan, sitting on her front verandah. The things she says turn into pictures in my own mind, things happen there.

Peas in a pod.
Drops of water like flowers.

Nothing could be more lovely to me than sitting here with Nan, Little Si playing beside. The three of us alone and nobody else to worry for.

The hot wind shudders through the pines, stops. Makes me think what the rain will feel like after all these weeks of dry. Will it be a refreshment? Perhaps a sign? When Jesus died, the storm clouds opened and it rained for three days before Mary could gather up his ghost and fly with him to heaven. Rain can be important to a person who waits for signs. It could mean summer's ending and everything will change.

★

Little Si thinks about none of these things. He runs around with the hose, filling up his paddling pool. Backwards and forwards to the tap, a little cut-out boy, just his underpants on, a leaf.

'Look at me, Nan! Look!'

He swings the pipe so the water flicks a necklace against the blue sky. He dances through it and the plastic tube flicks and turns. The water an arch for him, a circle, a window.

'I'm magicking! I'm magicking!'

He waves his arms and leaps through the water again.

'I'm swimming around the world, Nanny-Nan! Look at me!'

Nan shakes her head, she smiles. She reaches for the bowl of peas to start shelling. She could eat that child on toast, that's what she says.

Little Pixie Darling.

Little Pea.

When she cuddles him, she kisses his face all over, she nibbles at his ear like an old fish. She could bite his head clean off.

Little Si is her own favourite boy, my own brother. Perhaps this will be the holiday that we'll be able to stay here for ever with Nan and be our own complete family, just the three of us like in the Bible. A sign may never come that says we have to go home and we could stay here instead, quite safely, with Nan. The bowl of peas there for us to shell and no storm for trouble.

Last night in bed, that's what she talked about, about keeping us with her. How we could go to a little country school, if we liked. Have a lunch packed, with sandwiches and a piece of fruit and a cake to finish off with.

'Would you like that, honey? Come home here for your tea every day?'

I couldn't speak at first, it was so like a miracle. I'd been praying to God: Why should our mother want us back when the bad sickness is over? Wouldn't she like it more if she could be on her own? And us not there to bother her and make her ill? Nan said, 'Stay up here always, how would that be?'

And as I held her in bed, my arms tight around her body said *yes*. I wanted that wish so bad I could have broken with it. And if Little Si was older I know he would have wished for it too. *Please, please*. Let us stay. Change our names and be Nan's children. *Please, please*. Make the wish come true in heaven. In my mind's eye I saw all the white angels gathered with our bleeding Lord, but even then I couldn't stop the creeping spider thought: Does Nan mean it this time? Because why had she said it before, said we could live with her always, when it didn't come true? Why had she let us go home in the end?

*

I'm evil in that way, not believing hard enough for my prayers to come true. A person without sin knows that to truly believe, you must put yourself square in God's eye. Have Him see you and notice your wish. It's not enough just to pray for miracles, you must prove your love to have them come true. You must stretch the boy's throat back on the altar, your own son. Or perhaps it is an animal that must be killed . . . But always, in the Bible, it's the murders that make the wishes come true.

If you're stained and contain demons, it's not easy to try for miracles. When I clean up afterwards, I know it's my fault that our mother gets ill – she never wanted that baby. How can I pray when I spoiled her life? Her dances and balls and all her boyfriends? How can I pray now, torn out of her wedlock? When I'm the reason she's sick now, and frightening?

Nan says to give up on praying because it's all rot. She used to, she's stopped. She gave birth in a thunderstorm, a man she hated for a husband and a daughter man-sick. All these things come out in the songs she sings instead of hymns.

My roof's got a hole in it and I might drown.
There's whiskey in the jar.
Nobody knows the trouble I've seen.

★

All the songs have people hanging, wading in water, birds drowning. What do these signs mean? How much of these songs is true? Maybe there's a jump in the song, a joyful note. Nan might whistle the songs instead of sing them, but even then the pictures they contain are full of sadness. The earth crying, a baby born naked somewhere and left that way.

She sings these songs to us in bed at night, she never leaves us in the dark. Tonight, when the sky splits into rain and wind ghosts through the skinny old pines so their barks creak and moan, we'll be safe. We'll be inside the bedroom with the flowers on the wallpaper that look like little faces in the dark, with eyes and mouths, but kind. Nan will cuddle us up at her front and back, the blankets folded over and all the soft sheets. Little Si held in her lap like a cat or a plate of cakes or something else that you carry with gentleness.

Peas in a pod, sad babies.
Drops of water, grey goosedown but nowhere to sleep.

In bed, I pray hard to heaven that we can stay here in the room with the flowers. Pray that everything that Nan says will come true and that all the songs will have simple pictures with happy endings and no one killing the bird or causing that boy to hang. And we'd never go back, because from now on Nan would decide things, not our mother.

★

Pray, pray. Make her die, Jesus Christ. Snatch her to heaven. Don't let her come for us, like when she came the last time and took us away.

'Darling. Look how *tall* you are. How you've *grown*. How I've *missed* you looking after me.'

She wore red lipstick gashed across her mouth, and high pointy shoes. The tips of them went click-click as she walked across the floor.

'And my little boy, let me kiss him.'

Little Si was on Nan's lap, tucked under her cardigan. His face was hidden in her shoulder.

'We don't have to go back with you,' his voice was muffled from hiding. 'Nan says we don't have to.'

My mother looked at Nan, her eyes had a glint.

'What have you been saying to them?' She took a step forwards with her bent body, on her pointy high-heel shoes. 'What lies?'

At first Nan didn't say anything, she was stroking the hairs at Little Si's neck, that tender part. She was stroking.

Then she made her reply.

She said, 'No lies.'

She said it was just a story.

She said it was nothing that was ever meant to come true.

How my mother's red lips parted then. She smiled, she was so glamorous. She took my hand in her cool hand.

'I have presents,' she said. 'For my own two darlings. For

being so good and staying with their old grandmother while Mummy was sick.'

Her bracelets jangled as she searched in her bag amongst her cigarettes and the little bottle hiding there. She picked out two packets with papers that were bright and tinselly. Little Si peeped out of the cardigan, seeing the present that was to be his own. His hand reached out.

'But only if you kiss me first,' she said, she was walking towards him. 'Only presents when you kiss.'

Click, click. She was coming closer. Her hand containing the tinsel and bright paper, and Little Si still reaching. Later, his face would be smeared from chocolate and from crying, but for now he stretched out his hand towards her.

'My darling boy.'

She was using all her special loving words, all her jewellery was shining.

'My precious darling boy.'

There was nothing Nan could do to protect us.

But why am I thinking about these mean things now? When the blue sky's an apron? When Little Si is a boy carved out of a nut, running freely in the sunlight and his own paddling pool there for him?

'Watch me swim?'

He runs over to his pool, jumps in, thrashes there like a caught fish. His smile and shriek, and the trinkets of water all little hooks to keep us, caught and safe on God's line.

*

Nan looks up from the dish of peas, plucking out the peas from their neat homes and letting them drop.

'I'm watching, honey.'

She splits a pea like a trick, pops the pod into her mouth and swallows it whole.

'Just think,' she says to me. 'All this will pass. Grass, leaves. Our little piles of twigs . . . How they will wither. Everything to dust . . .'

She looks around herself, at all the bright day.

'We can't change things, you and I. We sit up here all day, under a bad sun, but we can't stop the weather turning. We make our piles of earth and they become graves around us. Nothing's as important as it seems.'

Across the garden, the hosepipe spins crazy water on the green grass. The glitter from the little pool could hurt your eyes. The red flowers lining Nan's paths and borders could hurt your eyes. Little Si's voice, calling out, calling to her, that could hurt you.

'Watch me swim, Nanny-Nan! Watch *me*!'

Nan loves Little Si because he's easy, just a stick. He's always been her own little boy, she's kept him safe and he's never had to pray to an angel or cut for blood to say sorry to Jesus. The red petals are thick on the path from where I picked them – but they wither under God's eye.

*

The world turns to dust, dust in the paddocks rising. Even the wet little boy out swimming had better cuddle up quick, he's another fish caught, safe but dying. Nan says she'll keep Si little for ever but one day he'll realize thoughts poke in.

The shelled peas are filling the bowl. Nan whistles the song about the poor Irish boy hung; she huddles against the weather turning. But now she can't always decide things and have them come true. She may know the storm will come for us tonight, banging on the roof, the wind hungry, but she can't know it all, only God, and He won't come back again unless I cut. In the darkness tonight I will reach for them.

I love you.
I love you.

Nobody will ever see us in the flower bedroom.

Nobody need ever learn who I am.

The meatyard

If he could just get it down, push down and break through the speed hold. If he could just –

Liner pressed his foot harder on the pedal, felt the metal through the rubber cut.

If he could just push down for that last inch.

He ground the heel of his foot in, pushed down the bony ball of his foot onto the cut rubber.

Harder.

But no good. The last half-inch of the pedal wouldn't fix, it wouldn't go any further, so Liner eased his foot up, tried one more time to press down but it made no difference now. The car was making full power, it wouldn't go any faster. It was full trip now, a whole empty road ahead of him wasted for real speed. The engine screamed at seventy miles on the clock; the car was too old.

That piece of metal couldn't take him where he was going shorter than the time he had to make the trip. Liner guessed anyhow that it would probably be time enough. Inside seventy for the road's length, an hour or so, then a couple for the summer hills beyond. He could be inside seventy, time enough. Now that he was on his way he was way in.

When he'd found the car this morning, getting to where he'd wanted seemed like a kind of dream. He couldn't believe it would come to him so easy. Old Man had him sworn he was grounded, locked into working at the summer place as sure as a chain fixing him from the backyard to the front door and Old Man had thrown away the key. Locked in by guilt chain to pulling weeds and concreting the front drive, wound up in heavy money promises to paint and mend the wrecked wooden fence that ran around the property, at night to shoot the live things that tried to get through the breaks. Rabbits, mostly, and small soft-hoofed deer.

He was stuck there, he had to do what he was told. Clean out the place inside with acid water, fresh whitewash the walls. Lay grass seeds, drive nails through the fence so at night when he'd skinned the dead animals he'd made, he could hang the pelts along it. That's where they dried for him, all through the hot night so he wouldn't have the smell. He could just leave them there, piled up one on top of the other, their cut-out shapes folded over the fence rim hard as cardboard. That way, the flat flesh side never had to show to him yet still he would have good proof of his killing for Old Man.

All summer he'd been kept grounded. With tests, grounded, with tasks that needed proof of completion. It was the usual bribe deal the father had going – this time: Do the work, make your money back. Keep the car. Lay off drinking and quit running the girls – especially the rich ones. You get back the cost of that thickly spilt expensive blood – and some. Then it's money time. No more wiping out a stranger between her legs, let some other sucker in – but that's the deal.

'Give me four months,' Old Man had told Liner. 'And then you can have it all back. The cheque is written out already and right now the garage is fitting a new carburettor into your Merc, new gearbox, the works . . .'
He'd looked at his son with the yellow inherited eyes the son looked back at him with. Bad-habit eyes, weak, with no true colour in the iris and the pupil black like a little hole.
'Give me four months and there's another cheque waiting for you too,' the father had said. 'It will set you up for good if you give me your promise on the deal.'

Liner just looked back, nothing left to say. It was too hot anyhow. He just shook his head like he didn't know anything, kicked his naked toes a little into the hard earth. He was already bought by Old Man. Already too much money had been used on him for the habit of taking it to rub out clean.
'Give me four months.'
And this time Liner nodded. His dark head, though it was bowed, meant to his father *Yes*.
Yes, I'll do it.
You've got me again.
Yes. Yes. Yes.

That was three months ago and he'd pretty much stuck to the deal, as liars go, pretty much held to his place on the dry lawn, a pile of new seeds in his palm to scatter on the scraped-out spread of grass, the shoots coming up when he watered them, and sometimes tiny wild flowers too. Besides, no good going too crazy when Old Man had spies all around the beach-front – his fishing buddies mostly, and some of his cocktail wives, and best of the lot the old boy he paid to keep an eye on the place, through winter when there was nobody there, more recently late summer and autumn too, and the spring. The paid one was the only real one to watch out for, Liner knew. Old Man didn't spend enough time at the summer place any more to earn real loyalty, and nobody would come stay at the cottage once his father had gained the habit of tacking dead animal skins to the walls, of keeping the meat bodies of deer and rabbit and sometimes wild boar strung up drying in the boatshed. Even so, Liner had to be careful. There were enough people left could still watch you, just the same. Even if they didn't come around the place, they would soon tell on him if they found out he was leaving too often, pulling out too easy on the deal. His father would come looking for him then.

Jesus, though, didn't he sometimes have to leave. There was the dried-up smell of old blood all through the closed-up cottage, some days and nights too rich, it made him gag. And it was the weather there, on the east coast, that mostly did it. The kind of weather that turned people away. You didn't get a blue summer that side of the country, you didn't get deep blue seas for swimming, one wave slipping a lovelier blue over the other, deeper and deeper blue into a sapphire distance. You didn't get a pretty sky. Instead it was nothing but grey, everywhere, water, sand, sky. 'Low air,' the locals called it. Hot and grey all through the summer. Still, unmoving air so humid it made the beaches damp, caused blackfly to breed in the undergrowth of bush, squirming larvae and buzzing black insects that would collect there in the wet leaves and fern roots, mass in thick swarms and grow but never really fly.

Four months, that's how long he was supposed to stick the place. Four months of grey heat and breeding blackfly and a sea that lay on the beach like a slab of iron. Four months of smelling damp on his sheets at night, on the pillow at his cheek. Four months of picking mould off the bread one day after it was bought. It was four months too long of being on his own, hearing his own breath in the still air, the pump of his own heart as he sat out on the old deckchair at midnight, the rifle laid across his lap, looking out for a pair of dark eyes shining through the gaps in the rotting fence, looking back at him.

It wasn't that he meant to give up the deal for good. He'd had mornings away already, and long afternoons, cutting loose in the boat to sail some way up the coast, spending time in the high street bar afternoons. It wasn't bad to cheat some days, he was born with that kind of small-lies mind. Besides, he would never risk losing out, not now when he'd already stuck around so long, and Old Man would be decent about the money, Liner could rely on that. He would keep his word, all the Daddies in that generation had generosity, they made sure there were plenty of zeros after the numbers they wrote. It was partly pride, partly wanting to get their sons really good.

All in all, Liner figured this wasn't deal-cutting now, it was more like time away. He was too greedy to give up the cash owed him for some dumb risk. So he waited until the race weekend, when everyone his father knew from the summer town would be headed up the coast to watch the yearlings run. That weekend would do it. Just a day or two away, hit one of the little hick towns south of the summer hills, hole up there for a few days, do the mean things he liked doing best.

To get there was easy, he had always been a clever puss for car stealing. Staying out for a couple of days, when his father had only left him enough small change for lager and beans and bread, was difficult to do. But he knew he could rely on charm and a knife, they'd worked before, and there was always money to be found with the poor country girls he'd get quickly and early. Once your pants were unzipped you were on the way to the bank. They always had money, poor girls, from working in the milk bar or helping dad out with the shearing. Even if it was just money jingling in the pockets of their little cotton dresses, that was okay, but more likely he'd find wads tucked into their lacy bras, into the elastic of their panties. There was always paper on them somewhere if the fix on them was good and tight and smart.

The thing was a risk, he knew, but Liner was too full of blood to change his ways now. He lifted the car easy from a summer short-stay who was renting next door. While the guy and his family were inside the tackle shop on the high street, buying up for a few days' fishing, Liner just slipped inside their sedan and twisted the wires. The engine caught in a second and he was round the corner and out of sight of the shop, and the half-dozen houses bunched around the sea front, before the visitors had even come outside onto the street with their hooks and wire, and tubs of shark gut and eels.

It was *too* easy. At first the car hadn't seemed a bad choice, bright racer-boy red, Japanese hatchback with brand new paint, the sort of car that a rich married fool just might buy to pretend to himself that he was more special than the suburbs. But as Liner turned the last corner to cut into the straight road that led inland, as he put the sea at his back and the dark blue of the summer hills clear in his windshield, he had the accelerator pedal flat on the floor and the engine was already holding at seventy. He pressed down some more – But it made no difference. He couldn't go any faster even when he wanted so badly to be free.

The nights had been worse than the days. Days he generally did what Old Man had prepared for him to do, laying wet concrete, getting the right anti-mould mix into the paint. He'd scrubbed down the woodwork inside, none of the cupboards cleaned properly since his mother's death. He'd put away in a bag some of the pretty things she had kept there – a set of bowls and plates with cherries painted on them, her embroidery threads tied different colours onto a wooden spool, packets of flowering seeds. He didn't throw the bag away because he couldn't do that, even though he was supposed to be clearing out for the money, neither he nor his father had been able to do anything like that for all the years. They were trying to keep close to her, he supposed, her room with her clothes in it still, the bed made up with the silk coverlet like any minute she might come in and lie on it.

Neither Old Man nor Liner could do a thing with his mother's possessions, they didn't feel entitled. Though she'd been a wife to one, a mother to the other, and intimate enough that both men had felt her fingers running through their fine hair, in comfort, or in affection, though they'd both felt her gentleness in the way she removed clothing from them, when the husband was too drunk or tired, and the boy exhausted from summer heat and long days spent playing at the beach alone – even so, that same woman hadn't given them the right to love her in return, for all their need.

Liner still wished for her a lot of the time. When he was sitting in some dark public bar in the middle of the afternoon, the sound of flies hitting up against a dirty window, and his yellow eyes closing in the heat. Or when the half-caste girls gathered around his car parked outside, passing their hands down its metal sides, giving him a slow looking.

'Can I get inside, eh?'

'Will you take me for a ride, handsome boy?'

And he'd taken them, and others too, whoever wanted it, and he'd left them all dumped on the roadside when he'd done and they hadn't even looked up at him as he drove away in his fancy car. And he'd missed his mother then, thinking about all the bad things he'd done with the women, the poor ones and the rich ones, the ones Old Man had wanted him to have but he'd only spoiled them too, and had to have the money to pay to get their insides cleaned out. And he missed her, too, when he was alone, picking mould off the bread, waiting for summer to end. Feeling the rifle laid in his lap as he watched for the small animals to come into the yard at night to be killed, missed her then, maybe, most of all.

He looked down the road. The dark summer hills were still ahead. And over them another small town, something else to do until Old Man found out, like he always found out in the end, but enough there to keep him busy in the meantime, until he sickened of himself and made it back home again. Who knows, maybe he'd sit pretty this time, like he'd never been away. Old Man might drive in from the city one morning and find Liner just sitting there out front, the dry grass razored close to the earth by the mower, the concrete of the drive smooth and hard. The fence would be mended so nothing could get through to eat his mother's flowers, and the animal skins would be drying along it as proof of a good job, and the dry carcasses shrivelling whole in the boatshed, the bones and eyes still in them, and the bullet, they would be proof.

'I got twenty this time, Dad,' Liner imagined himself saying. 'And I can get twenty more. All the skins you want to pin on your wall, Dad. Anything you want.' He imagined himself talking on and on, offering work, and not wanting money for any of it. 'Just let me help out.'

Liner realized he was dreaming. His yellow eyes looked into the blue hills ahead and he knew the man he was talking to in his mind was not his father, not a man with the same eyes, a man with little dark holes in his yellow eyes. It was the other member of the family he wanted to make the promises to. Her. His cut-off limb. He felt her cool cheek as she leaned over and kissed him goodnight, he heard his urgent whisper to her as he lay in bed in the dark, 'Please. Let me do something for you.' He was not like that any more, dreamer. Not any more a little boy under the sheet, still wet from swimming, salt in his hair. 'Please . . .' Now he was a man, with white dry feet dirty with blood and earth. And Old Man would be back for him, he knew it. His luck could never hold. Big money for a bit of summer work, big money for a few dead animals slung up on a fence. Big money always found out when the boys were cheating. An Old Man had nothing better to do than drive in from the city that weekend. He was lonely too. Of course he'd come sneaking in.

Liner shifted the car round a bend in the road and a white cross that someone had lashed to a fence post loomed up at him. Another highway killing was all. People were forever doing that, making little wooden crosses to mark the place of a death. Everyone drove on country roads too fast, inland especially. You wound up the speed for something to do when there was nothing else on the road before you. And then suddenly there it was, another car, a quick twist in the road you didn't know was there. This cross he came up close to now and passed had a name on it, most of them had names on them. Mother. Father. Son. Daughter. What difference did it make when they die in the end? What difference whether they lash your white cross on the side of the road or in a room smelling of old blood?

That smell was in the air now. It came straight off the abattoir ten miles up the road, old cooked blood. The smell of animals rounded up in trucks and lorries and driven to one place for killing. It was the smell he knew so well. Of his father's summer house. Blood money.

'Four months and the cheques are in your pocket.'

He had looked at Liner and the inherited eyes looked back at him.

'Four months and it's all yours.'

In the heat of the car, coming off the red-painted sides of the car, off the road, the air, was the smell of blood, and the money. In the heat coming off the steering wheel, in the hot sweat slick on his body, the wet on his fingers, in his palms, was blood. Inside the car he smelled the meatyard. He couldn't get past that smell. Though it was at his back, with the killed animals and the girls and the small towns, still it was before him too, even as he drove away, with him, everywhere around him, the animal smell. He didn't need that smell again. Like he didn't need the sound of meatyard animals shrieking in his ears, animals wounded from the bullets when he had only half-killed them, having to put three more in to finish off the job. Seeing the white eye roll. He didn't need any of it, the stink of skins left to hang, the scream like his scream when his father had to quickly close the door of his mother's room where something was hanging – 'That's not for you to see, son.' – in that place where they used to spend their summers, every year, when he had been a little boy.
'Four months and you're off the hook.'

No. He was on it.

Liner closed his yellow eyes. With no sight, he held the steering wheel in place, the nose of the car pointing straight down the road he knew by heart. He heard nothing but the engine's whine as he tried to push the speed some more, always wanting to be faster, holding his bony white foot down hard against the rubber pedal and the metal of the pedal cutting through because that's how badly he wanted to be free.

With his eyes closed you wouldn't see the yellow in them. Wouldn't know Liner to be the kind of boy he'd ended up showing to the town. He wouldn't be a cheater, with closed eyes, the type that stole from you or lied. He wouldn't be the type that touched a girl under her dress only to bring her on.

He pushed down on the rubber again, and the pedal clicked. The engine revved up to terrible speed. Liner kept his foot down and spun the steering wheel around hard. There was a noise, like something split clean away, then silence. When he opened his eyes the road was empty for miles and miles before him. He turned the key in the ignition and the car started again. He drove for some time, quite slowly, and after the last bend in the road the shapes and rooftops of the summer town came into view through his windscreen, in the distance but getting closer, settling in his vision, and the place his father owned was there.

Visitor

The dark house smelled of stomachs. Or maybe it was brains. But always it was the smell of offal cooking, always offal, that was nothing new. There were those soft transparent pieces bought cheap at the butcher's and left lying in pots of boiling water until they were cooked through and stinking. Their shiny sides gleamed from the plate, white crescents in pools of pale gravy, soft pink for lips and tongues.

That was the first thing, the smell of that dark house. Nothing seemed to have changed at all during the years away. Same closed-in house, same shameful smell. The green silk curtains at the window were pulled across the daylight, shading the sofas and tables and hump back chairs that crowded in the corners of the room. And outside, walking around in the garden, all the bushes and vegetables and huge bright flowers were just as I'd left them, arranged in plots but sprouting goblin arms of weeds from too much growing.

If you'd asked, I couldn't have said why I'd gone back at all. To that light so strong it stung your eyes and turned the grass into green glass. I wasn't there for a birthplace. Or for memories. People return to a place to see if they've left anything behind, they don't bring their accessories with them.

But how I was there with my little bag of outfits. I was wearing ripped jeans and a lipstick the colour of fire engines but the minute I stepped off the plane I felt the thin unprotective nature of my coatings. What was the use of any of it here? The bag containing my city things, the frocks and jackets and twinkling earrings, the special case for shampoo and creams. What use? When the light and heat and all the years roared up to meet me?

Tripping foolishly across the tarmac in expensive shoes, I thought: This is it, the old place. The blue sky was bearing down and all around the green hills rose and sang. Sun struck off the edges of things, off concrete, off aluminium, and in the long taxi ride to my Aunt's dark house the plastic on the car seats burned.

'Here for long?'
The cab driver chewed on a cigarette end like it was gum, the back of his neck seemed contented.
'Just two weeks.'
'Yeah? Long way to come for fourteen days.'

Two weeks was the time I'd given my boss at work, just two weeks. A short trip back, to check everything was okay. I owed it to Aunt Eila because she was old. It was the only time I'd ever taken a break from the job and she might not see me again.
'Just a visit,' I told the driver, and through the rips in the denim I could feel my skin.

*

My boss at work is a certain kind of man. Hires all the waitresses because he thinks he might sleep with them. Thinks he's Daddy, thinks we love him and honour and obey. I've held down the job for three years now, the tips are nice. Always you're behaving: the right smile at the right time, the confidential play of fingertips to prove everything's okay. 'I promise after two weeks I'll be back and it'll be like I never left.'

'Do you promise that you promise?'

I let my hands move against his in a way that could have made him think one day I would be his lover.

'Don't tell me you can't manage,' I said. 'Baby. It's only fourteen days.'

He put his arms around my shoulders, he was smiling. The lunchtime shift had ended and the cheques had been thick. He was, after all, a certain kind of man.

'As long as you come back then,' he said. 'As long as you don't stay there, take up your roots again, or some weird thing.'

I put my face in his neck, kissed him there on his little pulse.

'Just as long as you come home to me, darling,' he said.

Aunt Eila was still old and strong when I saw her again. Her letters had made it seem that she was nearly dying, with her friends boxed up and buried, and the garden run to weeds. But looking at her you'd never have known she'd been in the hospital at all. Her skinny arms were still muscly and brown as an old man's and she ran around the house in the quick, frightening way she'd always done when I was a child, growing up and knowing that other kids at school had fathers who went to work and mothers who wore stockings and lipstick and were pretty.

'A great old bird, your Aunt,' someone had said to me once, he was a person who had known my parents. He told me he'd brought a present for me that turned out to be a doll in a box with a set of clothes pinned to the cardboard behind her. He patted me on the head when he gave it, a hot and shiny man.

'Grow up like old Eila and you'll be alright in this world,' he said.

I held the doll in the box close to me like I loved it but really I'd been hoping he might have given me a photograph instead, of me as a baby and my parents holding me and smiling for the camera and being in love.

'Cat got your tongue?' Eila had her hand on me, grasping. There would be no photographs. She alone would be my familiar.

After the long taxi drive to the outskirts of town, it was late afternoon when I arrived back in her house. She was sitting in her favourite chair, at her needlepoint, as if I'd never been away. She moved and fiddled as she stitched the wool to its thick felt backing, callouses were eyes and noses.

★

'We've had a good summer here, this year.' Her voice came strong out of the darkened room, her fingers at the needle. 'You've caught the end of it but still it's deathly hot.'
Outside, the insects were busy. Prick, prick. Under every glossy leaf, they were nestling in thick, busy columns, worked up into the insides of flowers. Their wavering feelers and tiny wet heads would be working busily against the petals' edges.
'What a shame for you,' she said to me then. 'All the boys and girls out in their bathing things and, darling, you look so overheated.'
Prick, prick. She pulled the wool taut, made a knot, bit it clean from the backing with her teeth and all the time, as she worked, her body twitched with its own thoughts. Her whole body was alive with thoughts, thoughts glinted off the little pearls she'd always worn. Ideas about me were in her tiny bright eyes.

Years away from her, travelling back through days and nights and seasons – none of it could put space between here and then. I was hers again like I'd never left, my poor lipstick all undone.
'I have a good job there, Aunt E. I make lots of money. I live in a nice house with some nice people. I . . .'
She was threading up, another pig in a stable, another trapped plant for a cushion or a footstool. Her needlepoint in frames behind glass filled the silent spaces on the walls. Needlepoint at my back, my hard sofa.
'I . . . I . . .'

But why even try to speak? When her little pearls were eyeing me for lies? How to talk about my own life? The things I did to earn my money?

It's a very smart restaurant, the place where I work. I first noticed it because of the windows which are huge and opaque like they'd been dipped in milk. Outside the entrance was a stand of oriental trees, with thin, thin branches I'd never seen before. At night they were hung with tiny white fairy-tale lights that touched and glittered.

I started out as water boy, making sure the glasses were fresh, clearing plates. Some people say it's the hardest part of a restaurant job. Then, after weeks, my boss moved me up to waiting tables and I kept a tiny map tucked in my belt to remember the seating plan. There were special phrases – 'What can I do for you tonight?' – and different kinds of smiles. The money was good. Soon I could afford to buy shoes that were narrow and dark, shoes with long heels that I could wear at work because then I was taking more time, learning how to be a hostess and how to play.

I smiled at all the dark-haired men who were our customers. They were uniformly handsome with skin and eyes that were cleaned and buffed, their bodies encased in shirts and suits pressed into lines. Sometimes they brought their girlfriends to the restaurant with them, or their wives, and I smiled at them too, paid them little compliments. Other nights they were alone, late on a Monday, say, or a Wednesday, and then I would often go home with one of them. They kept hard beds, those men, but their lovemaking had a kind of liquidity that pleased me at the time. After it, I'd leave early, go home for my own sleep. I used to wake late in the afternoon, with ideas.

This was my life, my own chapters and sentences, no sing-song memories. There was no crying in it. Aunt Eila wrote me letters that arrived once a month like bleeding, but I'd trained myself to think less and less about the contents of my body and I could do it with her too. I had phrases for her that I used when people asked. *A sweet old thing*, I said. *Completely batty but always wonderful to me*. After a while, I realized the sentences were all I needed. I needn't think about her at all or the place where I used to live.

I felt safe. Like in a circus, with your own rules, safe like a box. I felt I was beginning a life, that I could be anybody. I really did believe I could step out, be so smart. A person might think, how young to believe that, a person might think, how vain. They would have known, wouldn't they, that eventually a letter would arrive, claiming me back. And didn't she say she was ill now, strung up with the operation. And didn't she hate the pills, hate the nurses, hate the day. Every word on the thin airmail paper crawled with intimacy; I was hers as if I really was a daughter. Why cheat myself that I had a chance to play with ropes, let myself be swung, when one day I'd be sitting in her darkness again, silent as a child.

'Should've brought your swimming things,' she said. 'What's the use of earrings or that bag of clothes now that you're home? Who's going to see you in fancy pants except me and I don't need impressing.'

She blindly lit another thread and bent again to the work. 'Remember me,' she said. 'I already know all about your skinny little body.'

A prick into tearing, that's how it starts. Remembering again. It's all happening again. Stepping off the plane, the air sucking up to meet you, can anyone avoid a homecoming? And things you see – a car window glinting in the sunlight, the fall of a piece of sky – remind you. Then you're plucking out an old woman's eyebrows, tweezering her chin. You're doing what you're told. Or you're standing up on a chair to fasten her bra before you yourself have got dressed for school. But you don't think it's so queer. None of these memories have to hold, you don't have to keep them banging in your head. Perhaps they never happened, you never did it, it's not real. Even the punishments she invented that were different every time, they could be just another sentence on the page.

And now, look at me. Now I'm the hostess. I'm the one who

greets. When people come into the restaurant I take their coats and show them to their tables as if it's my party they've been invited to. I wear the most beautiful things. At home, the flat I share is clean and light and painted in pale colours. The TV, video, telephone – all of it is modern. I spend hours talking to my friends about books and films and restaurants they've been to. I think about having my own boyfriend instead of letting my body get more messy with sex. Or maybe just stopping it. Maybe moving out and buying my own place. These things are my life, the thick pale carpets, scent, new shoes. So why did an old woman's gizzardy neck and threaded needle mean anything? What was my dressed body doing there, in a squint wooden house half strangled by tropical vines? Outside the shaded window, the hills and mountains were pressing in – but why claim me? What did my little outfits have to do with a country of mutton bones scattered through gardens? Of meat and fish heads wrapped in newspaper and buried in shallow graves?

On the plane, the stewardesses' faces had split with smiles through their suntans.

'How nice that you're coming home.'

Touching down, the forced air of the cabin pressed against the bright blue miles outside the window. I could see gorsy humpbacked hills, and the white mountain in the distance tipped into the churning sea. Even then, as the wheels spun and burned on the runway, I couldn't have told you why I'd chosen to be there. If you'd asked, I couldn't have told.

'Whew . . .' The overweight man at passport control whistled when he saw the date on my visa. 'Long time, no see, little girl.'

I grappled with my hand luggage, not looking for anything, just because the leather was so beautiful. New-looking and clean, even though it had travelled all that way.

'I'm only here for two weeks,' said my voice. 'It's only a holiday. It's only –'

'Hey, easy. I'm only asking, you know? Just relax.' He continued to finger my passport, licking, turning the pages over and over. When he came to the photograph, he looked at me, full on.

'All grown up, eh?'

My own face replied, *Please let me go*.

Kill them all. It's not as if I was there for a history, or for photos, or to find a set of memories I could keep. I didn't want a bit of their earth, the colour of their sky. I didn't need an aunt, dark house, the stink of unmentionable meats. I'd made myself forget about all that long since. Made myself, like being sick. Already I'd got rid of it, being an old woman's special kept and secret girl, I was nearly clean of it. Nor was there anything left in the house to remember me by. If you visited today, you would never know I had lived there. There would be no clues.

*

Even the photograph albums had empty pages. There were darker squares where the pictures had been and on some pages fragments of Sellotape lay like fingernails. And toys I'd played with – dolls – there was nothing in my old room. Since I'd gone she'd turned it into a kind of guest house, on the thin bed a blanket that she'd knitted herself from old scraps – not my own eiderdown, or any of my soft pillows. In the wardrobe there were just empty wire coat-hangers, a little ruined choir, no clothes, and the box at the top that had held the dressing-up things and my mother's wedding dress was stuffed full only of yellowing tissue paper.

Eila said she'd burnt everything because she couldn't stand it, that when I'd left she'd wanted me out, and that's how she'd done it. Made a fire and thrown everything in.

'You little bitch . . .'

I didn't mind what she said, I could forget it.

'Little animal.'

I didn't mind, didn't. The sound of a million screaming insects came from the vegetables and thick flowers and matted bushes where they lived. I didn't mind at all what she'd said. It would be an easy thing to change my ticket, be back at work the day after tomorrow like I'd never been away.

'Who do you think you are. Coming back here and expecting things? Who do you think wants to see you?'

She put down her tapestry and was looking. Her little pearls squinted at me off her chest. She still held the tiny needle.

'There's nobody wants to see you, and that's the answer. You've wasted all your money. All your fanciness, wasted.' She picked up her work again, she was exhausted, she was too old for tricks. I rose to make a cup of tea.

'It's been a good year here one way or another,' she said. 'A hot summer, the farmers are happy and so are my shares.' She looked at me then and I knew she'd be wanting to hold me, kiss me. 'I'm not ready to sell up yet. One day, darling. All this will be yours.'

The woolly thing in her lap heaved as she spoke. It was late afternoon and summer was ending for her. The green curtains hung like hair; the only light was a slice of yellow, like pollution, on the wall behind her head. Her curdled halo, it was what she deserved. Her end of summer, my spring.

I had always kept myself so quiet in that dark house, but now it was my turn for seed. I'd stayed virgin so long. Staying in that house, in that country, I'd waited out my time. Practising scales at the piano, removing my clothes for bed at night, cleaning plates after lunch. Once upon a time I was seventeen, and all the girls from school were wearing brown make-up on their faces and shining lipstick and mascara. They perched on the high spindly stools at the café-bar in Rubyleff's Department Store. Boys were there too, with tongues, but not for me. I kept myself so quiet in my own dark room.

★

Yet I was pretty, wasn't I? I could have been a star? I could have played in concert halls all over the world. Met my friends for lunch and gone shopping for clothes, items to wear. I could have been a daughter, found friends. Had a man to fall in love with and a wedding made of net curtains and pale gorse torn from the hills. If I'd wanted, I could have parted the curtains and let sunlight into the dark house, just for pleasure. I could have had the garden, its fevered flowers and bush, and the land beyond the clay gorge where the sheep tangled in branches and were caught, bleating, drowning in slimy mud when it rained.

I made Aunt Eila her cup of tea, milk and honey as she liked it. I stayed on with her for the two weeks, saw no one. I sat with her most days, indoors. The curtains were drawn and hushed while the weather outside was persistent, great loud crying blue days that never let up. My Aunt didn't say anything I would remember. She'd be dead soon anyhow.

I made one visit out. But the café-bar at Rubyleff's had been turned into a shoe department selling racks of socks and tights in ugly colours. There were no more spindly chairs where the girls had sat, twinkling under the chandeliers, filling their mouths with cream. There were no chairs where I had sat with Aunt Eila when she took me there for a treat when I was still too young to know better, to know that I was marking time in my dark bedroom, sleeping, keeping myself safe for leaving.

I don't know why I've chosen these things to talk about.
I'm a waitress in a bar.
I am the one who greets, the one who smiles at the customers as she takes their dark coats.
I wear expensive accessories, underthings.

I am that woman.

Everyone is sleeping

They turn in on the farm road not long before dawn. It's still dark, and they have no idea it will be morning soon, the sky is just the same now as before when they were driving. There's the same dark that was spread out in front of them on the empty roads, a darkness like ink poured across the windscreen when it rained. Later, when they stopped for petrol and coffee it was warmer for a while. The sky had cleared then and was blue as a jeweller's velvet with stars scattered across it like bits of glass.

'Yeah,' Sarah Jane said, when Carter was pointing out constellations to her, the Bear or the Belt, or the Plough.
'Can you see Orion?'
'I think so.'
'Can you see his arm?'

They were both standing leaning against the car, holding plastic cups of coffee with their heads craned back.
'If you connect that bright star up there to that row of little stars . . .' Carter was saying. 'Can you see? Just there where I'm pointing?'
Sarah Jane didn't reply.
'Look . . .'
He took her hand in his and used her finger to trace a shape. 'There,' he said, 'and there and there. Do you see it now? That little triangle of stars?'
'I think so.'

'Well, that's the Plough.'
'I see.'
But all the time he was standing next to her, though her hand was held gently in his, her finger pointing, she couldn't really see. It was just sky up there, just darkness.

They've only been travelling a few hours, and only have a couple of bags with them, some food picked up from a supermarket on the way, they have some wine – but it feels like much longer they've been sitting close beside each other in the car. It was cold when they left town, and there was the heavy rain that lasted for an hour or so, but when they turned off the main road Sarah Jane was able to put her head out the window for a while and feel the air on her face, the same way she used to when she was a little girl.

She used to love to be the passenger in her parents' car. She loved to sit in the back, with the window wound down and the warm air beating on her face. It was usually summer when they made the journey north, it was usually during the day, and from the back seat Sarah Jane could see everything, little towns, farms. Telegraph poles would flick by, fences, fields. She would count, one, for yellow fields, one two, for green. She could hear her parents' soft talking, like murmuring. There was the smell of the wide leather seats of the station wagon, the grassy, sunny air coming in through the open window.

★

She closed her eyes. She was happy then.

'What's so special about this place of yours?' Carter used to say, before she'd ever taken him on the same journey, through empty farmland, along the straight narrow roads. 'The country is the country, it's cows, it's sheep.'
'You'll see,' she said, and it was true, now he was the one saying after dinner in a restaurant on Friday night, 'Why don't we just go there, now?'
He'd bundled up his napkin, called for the bill. Already, she knew, he was imagining driving down the village road onto the farm, past the paddocks packed with clover and with grass. Turning into the woods, knowing there would be the square perfect lines of the house at the end of the road, the porch at the back, the planted flowers in the garden. She could tell, right then, by the way he drained his glass, pushed back his chair, how much he wanted to be there, within those empty rooms her father had made, walking in her mother's lovely garden.
'Why don't we just get in the car now?' he said, and Sarah Jane had licked her teaspoon, carefully licking the froth from the cappuccino off the teaspoon, before she answered.
'C'mon, baby, it'll be fun.'
And then she put down her spoon.
'Okay,' she said. 'But you'll have to be the one who drives.'

★

It's the only way she can do it now. Carter may want to come here more than she does, but she must be the only one who can look out the window to recognize the perfect pattern of the woods and grass, this part of the hills, the sheltered fold in the trees where a house was built. She holds within her the memory of this journey, drawn out for her like a constellation in the darkness, each element of the landscape connecting her along a line that is her past. Carter may want to come here now, but she's the one who belongs, on this road, under this piece of sky.

Let him drive.

She just wants to close her eyes into the air. Remember. There was the warm wind on her sunburnt face, the switch of dry grasses against the side of the car.

There in front of her were the backs of her parents' heads, her mother's smooth pale hair brushed back into a clasp, her father's collar like a band. There was the quietness of their voices. She remembers sometimes her mother would incline her head slightly towards her father, to whisper, perhaps, or to laugh at a private joke. Other times, if her mother was driving, her father would put his hand up to the back of her neck, to stroke it. He used his fingers, the heel of his palm. He was massaging her mother's neck, Sarah Jane knows this now, he was doing it to make her more comfortable, but then . . . She had to turn quickly away. There was something in the gesture that was more than itself, something she couldn't name. It was too sweet, too selfish for naming, as if she had found herself uninvited in the midst of the most private dream.

She opens her eyes.

All the years have passed and she is with Carter now, not her parents, it's his car they arrive in, his ugly Volvo tracking slowly down the farm road in the dark. There is the soft hum of the engine, the pitted crunch of the tyres over gravel . . . This is real, this is not a dream. Through the open window come the sweet familiar smells of the hill, cows out in the field somewhere, cut hay, and the lemony scent of a late summer flower which Sarah Jane remembers from all the times she's been coming to the house, a tiny seeded wild thing her mother loved.

Of course Carter was going to love it that he could come here, she'd taken his breath away with the beauty of the country that first time. He'd walked around the grounds of the house, looking at the plants and trees, exploring the woods, the path that ran alongside the river back up to the orchard and garden. She had opened the front door and he'd gone through all the rooms in the house, unchanged since her parents' death, he'd seen the bookshelves, the quilts and the curtains, the huge dresser in the hall with the collection of yellow and blue china . . . Everything was there, laid out in those rooms. Nothing else Carter would ever see in her could show, in the same way as the pictures chosen for her bedroom wall, in the vases for flowers set in exactly the places in the house you would need them, how she had been loved once, and how she had been so certain for a time that everything in the world had been made, like a perfect painting, for her pleasure.

She had planned it, that he would see it this way. That he would come to the house for the first time in high summer, that he would be completely taken in. Her mother's garden was still beautiful, though nobody tended it now, still the white roses tumbled on the lawn leading down to the river and the honeysuckle grew in a mass on the wooden archway of the back porch. She took him to stand under it with her, the curly yellow heads of the flowers all around them like a hundred little paper dragons putting out a hundred little red paper tongues. Carter had touched one of them, reverently as though it were a treasure in a shop or a museum. And Sarah Jane felt he was touching her.

'I can't believe it.'

It was like when they first started going out together, sleeping together, and he couldn't believe his luck. He'd never been to a house that was so prettily made, he said, so isolated and alone. He couldn't believe that there were woods all around the garden, that there was a river. He couldn't believe the beauty of the hills at the back of the house where they could walk, the paved courtyard at the side where they could sit at night, watching the pale light of the evening sky slowly fade.

She looks at his face now, lit slightly by the light of the dashboard. Nothing has changed for him. He's still as excited to be here as he was that first time. As the car passes the last of the farm buildings he lights a cigarette. She can guess what he's thinking.

He is thinking about the deer, hoping there are still deer in the woods.

He is wondering if they still come around the house at night.

Once, he remembers, he and Sarah Jane woke in the downstairs bedroom and there was a stag looking at them through the window. He remembers the image, like a photograph. The shape of the deer's antlers against the glass.

He wonders if she remembers that night, how quiet it was, how still. How she had woken him from a deep sleep, her mouth against his ear, whispering, *Look*.

★

They turn off the farm road and into the woods, onto Sarah Jane's own land, driving over the ruts and bumps and stones of the makeshift track and the tress are all around them now. The branches of the birch and alder are thick with autumn foliage, pale and crumpled in the artificial light of the car's headlamps, but Sarah Jane knows they will be yellow tomorrow and red and purple against the blue sky.

It's beautiful here, this time of year.

Even though she has been away for a while, still she knows exactly the colour the hills will be, how the river will be dark in the rocky shallows, thick with fallen leaves . . .

Still she thinks, *Yes*.

Everything here she knows.

She drives with Carter through the woods and it is as if she is the only one here, in this dark and most familiar place, as if everyone else in the world is sleeping. She feels deep in the midst of trees, totally alone. She puts her hand up, to her neck.

Yes.

★

The trees part in the channel of the car headlights, and seal closed behind her.

Carter drives carefully, slowly through the trees.

He may as well be on his own here.

Sarah Jane doesn't talk to him, or look at him, and though he usually loves driving, and coming down this tiny road, tonight his pleasure has been slowly draining away into her silence. He feels tired of the bumpy road, of the branches of too many trees hitting the side of the car. He only wants to get to the house, make up the bed and lie down – but he knows, now they're nearly here, Sarah Jane will want to do what she's done ever since she can remember, any minute now she's going to do it. She's going to ask for the car to be stopped, it will have to be in the right place, in front of the high hedge that marks out the beginning of the garden, and he will have to pull up there, and wait for her, just like her Daddy used to.

'Along here.'

Her head is turned away from him, looking out the window.

'Go more slowly.'

⋆

She barely spoke to him in the car driving up but now she acts like this little girl still getting her way after all these years, as if nothing has to change for her if she doesn't want it.
'Now,' she says to him, and he cuts the ignition.
'You sure you want to do this again?' Carter says. 'It's late, you're tired, we're both tired.'
She nods, she doesn't care.
'It's a million years you've been doing this,' he says, but she just gets out of the car, she leaves the door open. He watches her run lightly through the long grass to the gate.

She never tells him why she has to do these things. In the past she was quiet, and he didn't mind, when it seemed to be a quiet of intimacy that Carter loved, that began with his fingers tracing her brow and hairline, her closed eyelids, his fingers pressed across her lips . . . Now he knows her silence is nothing like reserve. It's not shyness or sex. It's like the silence of a river, something held back from him, like a channel, a deep reservoir formed in herself and she won't let the water go.

'Five minutes,' she calls out to him, and Carter leans over and closes the door.

He remembers when they first met, her dark eyes, her smooth hair lying on her shoulders. He remembers the way she looked at him, and there were secrets in her eyes or sadness, and he wanted to be the one who would take care, who she would tell all her secrets to.

But she never tells. He sees her out there by the gate, blanched in the headlights and there's the familiarity of her body and her face – but no trace of him is there. She's like a map with no places marked on her and yet everywhere boundaries and rivers and seas.

He puts his hand up to the back of his neck to rub it, he rubs his tired gritty eyes.

She walks the last few paces to the gate and unlocks it with her keys.

She always keeps the keys, she thinks she will never give the keys away.

She uses one of them to unlock the gate, but she doesn't open the gate just yet, she leaves the key in the padlock, the others hanging from it on a chain. This is the part that Carter wanted her to forget about, because it's late, but she can't forget, it's part of her, no matter how late it is. She will lean against the gatepost as she's always done and look down the drive towards the house.

★

'I wonder who lives here.'

It was a game her mother used to play. Her father would have to stay in the car, and her mother would take Sarah Jane by the hand and together they would go to the gate, they would unlock the padlock, and lean on the gatepost, looking at the house down the drive.

'What a lovely place to live.'

They would be standing there together at the edge of the garden, they would look at each other and smile. Then they would walk through the garden to the house, they would peer into the windows.

Her mother would whisper, 'I wonder who lives here.'

'Look,' she would point through the glass. 'They must have a little girl too, just like you. See, she's left her doll there on the sofa, and that book – isn't that one of the books you like?'

Sarah Jane remembers every detail of the game as if it's happening now. Her mother's face, the feel of her cool dry hand. It was like a memory that had been made, piece by piece the most perfect, perfect memory that she would have to live with for the rest of her life.

'They must have a little girl, too.'
'Look.'

She looks across at the little house, like a child's drawing of a house her parents made. It's like a sign, a perfect image of their secret life together, their intimacy creating walls and chimneys and gardens and pretending a child could share it with them.

Sarah Jane shivers. The air is dark and cold and richly scented with something ploughed into the farmer's field, silage, a thick wet growth of grass cut and left lying to sweeten and rot for winter feed.

'I wonder who lives here.'

She pulls her jacket close around her.

'Might it be someone like you?'

Long minutes have passed by now. The velvet of the sky is slowly tearing open to show the purple and silver light of dawn. In the car, Carter yawns, rubs his neck, his gritty tired eyes. Finally Sarah Jane pushes the gate open so he can drive through, and as he swings the car around towards the garage at the back for a second, the headlights reflect in the front windows of the house, make it seem as if there are people there already, a family, as if the house might be warm, and full of sound and light.

Then the driveway curves, the house is dark again.

He guides the car into the garage porch, turns off the ignition. He switches off the lights. It feels as if he's been driving days and nights to get here, much longer than he remembered. He wants to go to sleep. He grabs the two bags from the back seat and starts walking towards the front door.

He can't see Sarah Jane anywhere.

Minute by minute the darkness is lifting. He looks down the drive, into the garden by the field but he can't see her. He wonders if she's inside the house, walking around on her own in there. But when he gets to the front door it's still locked.

He puts the bags down and goes back to the car for the rest of the stuff, the groceries, the box of wine and beer and juice. He brings it all around and piles everything together, by the tree at the front door.

He calls out, 'I'm ready! Bring the keys!' but his voice just hangs in the air.

He wonders how long it was since they were last here. He's

trying to remember whether she ran off like this last time, or was it daytime when they came? Was it summer?

He can't remember. The front door has moss growing up it and they haven't scraped it off, perhaps it was a summer long ago. The branches of the tree are too long, they lean over to touch the door, he'll cut them back if Sarah Jane will let him. He walks out onto the lawn; wild flowers and weeds cover the pathway, and the grass is high, up to his knees, the whole sweet place overgrown and sad.

He calls again, 'C'mon, darling . . .' but there's no answer. He goes back to the front door and sits down on the little bench beside the tree to wait.

She could be anywhere, she could take all the time she wants. She's in charge here, she can cut the grass, leave the grass, let damp come in, let the house slowly rot and die. She can do that. She can leave him to wait for her by the door, he can wait and wait and she can take as much time as she wants before she comes to him or not – she can do that too.

The bench seems hard, cold. It's her bench. Everything here is her property, the place she is hiding herself in now, down by the side of the house somewhere, in the orchard maybe, hidden in trees at the edge of the woods.

★

He's so tired.

They have everything they need here, with this land, the hills to walk on. They could have it, the two of them, they could claim it as their own. They could be happy here, bring children here.

He could sleep under the trees in the orchard and hear the voices of others in the garden around him.

He closes his eyes.

He could be sleeping now.

Sarah Jane sees him from where she stands amongst the trees at the bottom of her garden.

He's sitting in front of her house with their bags at his feet. His head is bowed.

He looks cold. The house looks cold, cold and silent as if no one had ever lived there, had holidays there. The front door is locked, as if no one has ever been inside, opened windows, lit fires. As if no one has ever woken in a room there and walked outside in the early morning, sipping coffee from a blue and yellow cup.

★

It is empty, everything is empty.

Wherever she looks, through the thin trees across the garden, to the house, there's nothing. There are the walls of a building, some windows, one with broken glass. A patch of grass overgrown with weeds.

I wonder who lives here.

Nothing.

Only images, a child's drawing. The garden where her mother used to walk, clipping back the long stems, the rooms where her father kept his books, dark now behind the broken glass . . . It's only images of her life that inhabit this place now and she is the visitor of the game. She sees her father, taking a book down from a shelf, opening it and beginning to read as he walks to his chair. She sees her mother, alone on the smooth lawn, the neat cut of the pruning scissors against the thin branch. She's at the window, at the fenceline, at the door. She was always just the visitor here.

'Tell me what you're thinking,' Carter used to say. 'Tell me your secrets.'

But how can she tell him, after so many years have passed, that this is all she is, the one who stands aside, who waits to be invited in? How can she, after all their time together, tell him now, that what she keeps from him is the only thing about herself she knows?

She remembers the way her father would leave his chair, her mother come inside. There was the way they used to find each other in the house, the way they closed the windows and the doors behind them.

The way her father put his hand up to touch her mother's neck.

She turns, she covers her eyes.

'Where are you?'

She can hear Carter calling from across the garden, and she knows he's cold, wants to go inside, but how can she go to him, answer him?

'Tell me your secrets,' he used to say.

And she wants to, she wants to go to him, put her arms around him, in these last small, dark minutes before dawn, she wants to comfort him, take him indoors, lay sheets on the bed and they can lie there together. But how can she be close to him, how ever tell him that she can't even come near him, without the memory of some other kiss or touch? That it's only the past that she has in her possession, nothing more, like the house he thinks she loves, nothing lives inside her and she's empty and cold and dry.

'Where are you?'

She can hear him, calling for her across the dark.

'Sweetheart, where are you? Please come in.'

But she can't leave her thin place by the trees.

Carter calls again, 'Please, Sarah Jane, wherever you are . . .' and then he gets up from the bench. He leaves the bags. It seems hopeless to him. All at once, in this cold, it's hopeless. He fingers the car keys in his pocket, starts walking towards the garage, then for no reason he turns the other way, towards the gate, into the field. He climbs over the gate and stops, he doesn't know where he's going. He just wants to be away, neither here, nor driving, just to be nowhere. Let her stay, he thinks, in her orchard, in her garden, wherever she is hiding. Let her stay, let her keep herself hidden from him, if it's what she wants he wants it, it makes no difference, and the relief of that thought, suddenly now it's come to him, is like breath, it's like being able to breathe again.

*

I don't care!

He wants to put back his head and cry, I don't care what you do! He wants to howl, like an animal, into the sky, I don't care! I don't care! But he's tired, starts towards the car again, and then he stops.

There at the edge of the wood, the deer have gathered.

He can't see them clearly, but they are there, the soft brown shapes woven in among the trees.

Carter doesn't move, he stays exactly where he is.

There is the arch of their dark heads, the thin stems of their legs as they stand together, the pattern of their antlers, like branches against the trees.

He is so close to them, it's like that other time.

Look.

Sarah Jane had woken him, she had whispered in his ear.

See how beautiful he is.

*

From the orchard where she has hidden herself she sees Carter now, so quiet and still.

Just like that other time, he's so close.

Look.

He doesn't move. The deer don't move.

She had whispered to him, and she could feel her breath against his ear, she could feel him lying next to her, the touch of his body against her skin.

Look.

It's only her that separates them.
Only her fence, her field, her garden.

She sees the deer motionless before him, gathered close together like a silent chorus. They are waiting to see what he will do.

Everything is still, the field, the flowers.

Still, like a painting, made, like a painting, to give pleasure.

For Carter it's like he's in a dream. He stands so quietly he can feel every particle of his body, the planes and edges of his body suspended in time, alive and sensitive to the tiniest movement, the slightest breath . . .

Look.

She was so close to him, there was the texture of her dry lips against his skin, her mouth, her warm breath . . .

Look.

The memory shivers through him.

She looks at the keys to the house in her hand, she looks at her house, her fence, her garden.

She puts the keys in her pocket, she starts walking towards him.

Look.

He woke, and his warm body was against her body.

Look.

She starts to run.

He loves her so much, there's nothing he can do, sex or words or money or food can't show it. Nothing in him is enough to express the feeling he has towards her. Unspeakable tenderness and nothing he can do with it.

He hears a sound, moves. The deer scatter.

He turns, and he sees her running towards him. There is the torn sky behind her, above her, the light is coming but there is time. She is calling to him, running towards him, she's calling his name.

The animals are in the field. Cows, a tiny calf set in the grass. There are wild cornflowers, autumn flowers. Everything is still, like a painting.

The keys drop from her pocket, she hears them fall into the long grass, amongst the flowers.

Still she runs, running across the lawn, across the field towards him, calling out again her husband's name.

Jesus, I know that guy

You hear things, don't you? Or see them with your own eyes. Some people I know even take a newspaper, they catch up that way. Me, I'm an old tom-cat. I take things in anyhow. Stare them out, sniff around a bit. Lick out the muck. Whatever way you look at it, bits of life are scrabbled all over the place . . . Empties spilling from plastic bags, two people. Nakedness. It's all happening out there in separate pieces, but you'd have to be a white-eye not to see the connections.

I mean, I'm a regular guy. Things happen to me too. Wanting to get the boot in, for example, when one of my so-called friends starts tipping at me over my drinking. Vodka, mind you, and everyone knows the clear stuff doesn't hurt anyone. No sir, not so far as I'm concerned. I'll take it down straight with a cold Nescafé chaser, feel the stomach slide open for it then close. No fiddling with lemonade, no squirt of cherry-coloured mixer for me, no way.

So this is one of my so-called friends doing the talking, yippety-yap, over a spaghetti bolognese down in my favourite local fairy-lights and rubber-plants Italian. It's the liver, the kidneys. It's not having a wife. Apparently the old Stoli was waltzing away with my life and I hadn't even checked my dance card yet. Well, I took it, I guess, for about twenty minutes, mopping up tomato sauce all the while, ear cocked, crumbling bread-sticks. 'Yeah,' I kept saying to my so-called. 'Yeah.'

*

It was getting late. The Italian brothers dimmed the lights and brought out dripping red candles. We were hooked into lovers' hour. All around us, young softies fondled each other over the checked tablecloths: they stroked and wiggled and I noticed none of them were working their forks too hard. I certainly could have done something with those fettuccines, could have handled the odd tortellini parcel – but then, I wasn't in love. My empty plate said that.

It didn't matter how many candles were flickering at me, or how many fairy lights were performing a romantic routine in pink and green, I still had old you-know-who shovelling lasagne and nineteen-to-the-dozening me over my habits with the spirit of Russia. Jesus. It would make any strong man puke – let alone me – and I'm so skinny you could thread me through the eye of a needle.
Still, 'Yeah,' I kept saying, and 'Yeah.'

We'd been through two crème caramels and were sugaring our coffees before his mouth clamped onto what he really wanted to talk about: me and that girl I used to run with and why I'd let her go.

'She was cute-looking and she had a nice little nature.' He took a sip of coffee, his mouth puckered up like a kiss. 'You could have married her, that's my belief,' he said. 'Had babies and a proper job. Your life could have changed. You could be in this place spooning custard to the tots and playing a little footsie with a wife of your own and instead you're here with me.'

He was on the nail, of course. That woman I used to be with, the things we used to do. It was another piece of the picture altogether. I'd been a different man then, hanging around the stockings section of the big department stores, passing my hands through filmy ribbons of suntan and nude, feeling knit up to something that was actually entirely separate from my own life. The stocking legs that hung from my bathroom rail, the filled-out, plump and shining legs that wrapped around my neck, being close, that close to all her odours. Well, these were things no longer contained in my day.

'Yeah, yeah.' My coffee was bitter. 'Maybe I should have married her, moved in, whatever men do.' Who knows, maybe we could have sprung a generation. She could have unhooked her bra in front of me every hot night, I could have made her fancy meals on a tray. Other times, just laying her down would have been soothing enough, going over and over the rounds of her body. Prising her open, like a shell, whenever I wanted her. Jesus Christ. The world could have been my bloody oyster.

Could have been, mind you. And that's one big mother of a conditional. Because who's to say she wanted me in the same way? After all, she left me, didn't she? Maybe I didn't try too hard to get her to stay but what words are there for begging? Please? Don't go, honey? They're crippled halfwits, those sentences, and besides, who uses a lot of words in a friendship anyway? You run out of things to say pretty early on, that's my experience. Sure, you start off thick enough, so many words you could gag on them. The facts, and the sentences – and the sticky tears. Out it comes, out it all comes, the fat story of your life but before you know it you've talked your guts out and there's nothing left to say. You go to her, to confide, and choke up air.

'Had a good day?' is what you're left with.

'That's a nice dress.'

You're looking at her, your hand passing over the soft tops of her legs where the nylon ceases to bind, and that's all you can say. It's the same, the nakedness of the two of you together, but the other thing has changed. Your words have turned into strangers and you try, but there's no need to speak any more. 'I love you, honey,' maybe.

Or, 'Please don't go.'

Hell, she knows why you chew your nails, why your eyes are blue one day, black the next. And all you want to do then is curl yourself with her, snug like a worm, lay your pumping head down in her lap. Have her caress you, be kind. No words because both of you are bodies, wrapping and unwrapping, there's eloquence in your embracings. Eyes closed, you realize everything you've ever wanted to say is right there.

*

I looked over at my so-called friend and realized I'd been out daisy-chaining. How things were, could have been. Alternative lives. Spinning some old yarn in my head while the real stuff ran right along beside. I was in her arms, being kissed by her long, cool tongue while two ropey old guys who used to like each other sat deep inside some spaghetti house.

His coffee done, he called for the bill.

I looked at him, keen. 'Want to come back to my place for a swifty?'

He shook his head. 'Not tonight, Josephine.'

'Just a lick?'

'I for one,' he said, 'don't want to punch my liver in.'

He shook his head again, dry croaker that he really was. 'If you had any sense you'd lay off too,' he said.

I had a clean bottle at home, just sitting there, freezing. Even the top was un-notched.

'One drink,' I said, pulling out the old begging words. 'It won't kill us.'

He'd picked up a teaspoon and was fiddling with it. 'One drink, three drinks,' he said. 'Next thing you know the bottle's dry and we're on the floor.'

'Think of it,' I was set to try it one more time. 'The bottle icing up. You know, I put it there for you.'

*

It was no good. Even as I spoke, I knew the thing was killed. He'd go home to his wife and children like he'd planned all along and I'd be back at my place, lifting the Stoli out of the freezer, feeling the oily plug of the drink seal my night. How it would pour, slow and pure, into my clear alone glass. Even as the begging words carried on in my head, grabbing my friend's sleeve, smiling in a sickly way, I knew it was over, the evening, the next day taken care of like a patient. The next twenty-four hours would surely see me walking down some street somewhere, trawling rubbish in the gutters, hung-over and belly-sick at what I'd done to myself the night before. I could see myself already, squinted up against the diesely gas of summer sunshine, walking west, home again, straight into the face of a swollen fiery sun and feeling like hell. The light would shimmer, so bright my pinhead eyes wouldn't be able to take it in. Only glints, colours.

But just because I could only pick up bits of the picture didn't mean other people couldn't see me, the whole thing. They might stare, thinking God knows what. And maybe the woman I spent time with back then, maybe she, quite complete with her own life, with a new set of clothes, make-up on that turned her eyelids into little blue moths. She might see me too. Might think, as her eyes fluttered, landed for a second on my dank clothes: *Jesus, I know that guy.* Then walk on.

Tinsel bright

Years before Moma divorced my Dad he used to dress up as a fairy for the hospital every Christmas Day. In that role he was truly beautiful to see. A blond man, and delicately made, he stunned all the patients with his wide variety of fairy outfits, a froth of tulle and sequins, in colours that I would have chosen, if I could have been a fairy too.

This, of course, would never happen. Only doctors were allowed to wear the pretty tutus and the tight spangled bodices with fitted bra. It was the custom at Victoria Grand, the hospital where my father worked as a heart surgeon, for the men to transform themselves this way. For more than fifty years they had tripped the bright wards as elves and pixies on December the 25th, spreading cheer and good humour to even those so ill they couldn't laugh out loud, couldn't leave their beds. It was my Dad's arrival at the hospital, however, that made the event really special. From his first parade he'd seen the limitations in the green cotton costumes, his red elf tights had chafed him badly and carried the smell of too many wearings.

'As there is no doubt that the annual parade is of enormous benefit to all the patients at Victoria Grand, I would like to suggest we make the event even more entertaining,' he'd announced to the Social Board, quite soon after his first Christmas. 'Therefore, if you'll let me, I'd like to make our parade a Spectacular. I'd like to be in charge of costumes from now on.'

*

I was perhaps five or six then. I remember it well as being a time of outfits. My new school required that I be dressed in a variety of uniforms, pale blue linen dresses for summer, serge pinafores with blue flannel blouses when the months were cool. My mother took me shopping in a special uniform shop and I came home with boxes of blue blazers, coats, hats. There were brown socks and white socks and three different kinds of shoes. Yet, though I loved taking the things from their paper packets, smelling the newness of fabric and leather, none of the clothes pleased me as much, when I put them on, as I hoped. None of them were fairy.

In the meantime, my Dad toiled at the sewing machine, and was planning, planning. What I know now is that the magic of these Christmases past, in the sparkle of a sequinned bodice, in the stiffened folds of a sugar-pink gown, comes from it being a time when doctors were men and men only. Girls didn't dress up and play this game. Even the pretty nurses looked lumpen and unhappy when compared to the sight of senior staff on parade. Giggling, they nudged each other when my Dad darted past them with his tinsel wand. They knew that, with his first Spectacular, 'Fairies from Foreign Lands', he'd started something different. It was only the beginning. 'Fairy Friends of Aladdin' he announced the next year. Then 'Winter Fairies in the Snow'. 'See this trimming, Francie?' He'd lengthen out a piece of bright silver for me to see, but never touch. 'I'm going to stitch it to the hem so it looks like ice.'

★

Still, even though things may have looked like a hospital romance movie, with handsome men treading the wards and a nurse by their side, my own mother was no sister. She was a painter, just starting out when I was born but there were big plans for her career, I know. All through the 1960s she was friends with Clement Greenberg and Franz Kline and Helen Frankenthaler, as well as some famous dealers in Paris and Berlin. We called her MOMA after the gallery in New York City, her favourite place in the whole wide world. I think she liked that. I think it helped her believe things would work out alright for her in the end.

Whatever, it was surely her tenderness with colour that got my Dad falling in love. He'd always wanted to work in the theatre. The heart-doctoring was his father's idea, he said, not his, and it had saddened him ever since that he'd let himself be bullied into following a career he didn't care for. 'Don't ever listen to what parents say,' he used to tell me. 'That's my advice. You've got your own life to live and your mother and I don't feature in it, believe me. Follow your instincts, Francie. I wanted costume! Costume! The smell of greasepaint in the air! Now all I have is a Christmas show once a year. I'm a sad man.'

Oh, but I didn't believe him. My Dad smiled too much, tickled me too much, to be unhappy. Besides, he'd invented the Victoria Grand Fairy Day, hadn't he? How could the sight of more than twenty doctors, all fully outfitted by the skill of his hands, be sad? Even when Christmas was months away I'd come into his study and find him with the wooden chest out, armloads of fabric and stockings and tinsel wings spread around him. He used to do his own make-up too, practising different 'looks' well in advance of the big day. In all my life I have never known a person possess more cosmetics and lotions; he almost had too many bottles, jars, creams.

Still, these kinds of thoughts did not flourish then; these were the fine days of my mother's talent. Her studio seemed always filled with light and the pleasant sound of her humming as she worked. Moma wore a yellow smock for painting, we were all three of us in costume of one sort or another. Blotched bright all over her front were the colours she used: vermilion, emerald, clear sea blue. They formed a pattern there, as if she too was a pretty canvas. Her cheeks might be smudged with paint; she would have stepped back from her work to consider it, resting her face in her hands, thinking. I knew that gesture well. She was so calm and lovely then. When she took her hands away, colour was there.

How different that unconscious mark upon her from the painstaking detail that went into my father's Christmas face. First he creamed his cheeks and brow, smoothing the shadows away from under his eyes and carrying the pale colour all the way down from temple to jawline. Only when his features were blank and perfect as one of my mother's new canvases did he begin the detailed work: drawing in the fine line of black that outlined his eyes, painting over the lids a film of shimmering blue. He filled his pale eyebrows in until they were dark and exciting-looking and after he had coloured his lips a juicy red he used Vaseline to make them shiny and wet. 'Cherry ripe,' he used to say.

By contrast, Moma in her studio worked earnestly in flat colours. With a broad knife she scooped up the thick oil from her palette and spread it like softened butter across the canvas, working the pigment in with the palm of her hand until the whole surface was deeply stained. The clean scent of her work rose from the floor where she was crouched over it, painting the last quick lines that were her signature. Without looking up she'd say 'Hi' when I came in. 'Had a good day at school? Miss me while you were there?'

These things, as I remember them, seem like nice times for a girl. Even my Dad working late most nights didn't disturb the impression we three were happy together. Moma and I ate our supper at the big table in the dining room, waiting, listening, like a TV family, for the sound of his car in the driveway. Then when he walked in the door we both ran up and kissed him and he put his arms around us and called us 'my girls'.

'What have my two girls been doing today?'
'How's my big girl?'
'How's my little girl?'
As he sat at the table, eating the meal Moma had kept warm for him in the hostess tray, I watched my parents together. My mother, changed into a new dress for the evening, the scent of linseed warm like fragrance on her skin and my Dad sometimes reaching out to take her hand, to stroke it. How I loved it when he did that to Moma, and how she seemed to need it too. She put her own hand over his, then leaned over and kissed him on the mouth.
Cherry ripe.

All wives were behaving that way towards husbands in the early sixties. That was what my mother said, much later, when everything had changed.
'We were putting up, darling. We were dealing, but that's all we were doing. I was an innocent when you were young. I had no idea your father was the way he was. No one will understand this now but when I married him I really believed he would be a husband. All the fairy days were nothing to me, I believed, I believed.'
I was grown-up by then but still I put my hands to my ears and ran from the room like a little girl. I too had glimpsed my father beneath his white doctor's coat, knew how manly his dark suit had been.
'All the time he was lying to me,' my mother, in the next

room, talked on. I put a pillow over my head but even then could hear the sound of her, talking to herself maybe but the words coming to find rest in me. 'I never knew . . . I never guessed. Now my life is over and I feel like such a fool . . .'

From now on, I guess she'll always be that kind of woman. Yet there was a time when she had a family, a career, and a turkey to slice when my Dad's fairy parade was done. It took me to change all that, the quiet daughter you should never trust. We could have had Christmas Days the same for ever had it not been for that one day, the last, had it not been for me.

I was ten years old. I remember because the parade dresses were based on *Swan Lake* which my Dad had taken me to see earlier in the year for a birthday treat. When we came out of the dark matinée theatre into the brightness of the afternoon, his eyes were shining.

'That's it, Francie! This year I'll do white tulle and swans-down. I'll make the dresses ankle-length and petticoat them so they come out to here.' He swept his arms around him in a circle. 'What do you think?'

In the months that followed he worked hard on the idea, in the evenings drawing up patterns for different designs, then experimenting with cloth, cut, and sewing right up to the weekend before Christmas Day when suddenly the dresses were nearly done and he was stitching white beads onto the bodices, a thick crust of them like frost, and all by hand.

Although when they were finished they were to me not as beautiful on the bulky forms of the doctors as they had been on the ballerinas in the theatre, still my Dad was so slim in his gown he was dainty. He'd put on a special cream that looked plain white in the jar until he dipped his fingers in and they came out sparkling with a million trillion glittery bits. Gently, he applied these to his cheekbones, his throat, his shoulders, patting the cream down so the tiny stars became affixed. When he took up his wand, and turned, twinkling in the light, my heart stopped. If a real fairy had asked me what I wanted most in the world, I would have wished for a pot of that glitter. More than any of my Dad's outfits or silver shoes, I wanted my fingers deep in the jar, to bring them out rich with stars.

Christmas that year we had a guest in the house. He was a colleague, my Dad said, 'On Loan'. He came all the way from another hospital up north and it was my Dad's job to show him around Victoria Grand, teach him about hearts. He was a tall man, I remember, and completely bald, the skin stretched tight over his forehead and head taut and shiny as a sheath.

'Your Dad looks great, doesn't he?'

I was watching the parade with him in the hospital. I was even holding his hand. Across the ward, my Dad was running around the beds with the other doctors just like they did every year.

'Twinkle, twinkle!' they called out to the sick and dying. 'Happy Christmas to you!'

As usual, it seemed everyone was laughing, even if they couldn't sit up in bed properly, patients loved my Dad's Christmas show.

'I'll make your wish come true!' one fairy doctor said to an old lady lying on her back. 'I'm your little bit of Christmas magic.' He pirouetted for her and though she couldn't move her head at all, I saw that she was smiling. 'Happy Christmas to you.'

In the midst of all the swan dresses and the dancing I saw my Dad looking around, looking for me I thought, at first, but it was the man whose hand I held he was seeking. When he found him, their eyes met. He smiled. For seconds, it seemed a lifetime to me, they were held together in stillness amidst all the bright whirl of the room, the swirl of white organza skirts, the laughter. Then my Dad came running over to us and tapped us both upon the shoulder with his tinsel wand. That was all he did. Yet, though I was left bare of his touch, a fragment of the wand's silver stayed on the man's jacket, glittering. Then I knew. Knew enough to watch them for the rest of the morning, watch them when we went home to my mother's turkey meal, watch them in the bathroom together, my father pretending to take his make-up off, the other following. Through the crack of the door I saw them with each other, the expert speed of their hands, placement of kisses, my Dad's wet mouth.

Cherry ripe.
I'm the guilty one who told my Moma all.

Today, I don't call her Moma. I use her real name, Marjorie, when we talk on the telephone. She tells me about her job in the art supplies shop, the people she meets. Her own painting she gave up on years ago, I'm not sure that she writes letters to art magazines and painters, or does any of that stuff any more. Even so, she seems pleased enough with her life.
'Contented,' she says.
She still wants to talk about her marriage years with me but even now I can't hear any of it.
'You should get in touch with your father,' she tells me. 'You know, he and I have found friendship over the years, I'm sure you could too.'

After my Dad left home I couldn't talk to anyone for a long time. Now I understand why he so loved the theatre, the costumes and disguise, but it took me a while to discover that. The more layers you can dress yourself in the safer you become, and quieter. Years later, and, like him, I've become a doctor, I specialize in hearts. When I started out in medical school I couldn't so much as dissect a soft mouse or any kind of rodent, but now that I'm fully adult, in my own dark suits, and white coat, I can snip and snip and snip. Although I have many friends, play tennis and go out on dinner dates most weekends, I am actually a very lonely person: unlike my Dad,

I lack the real ability to transform. When he sent for his clothes, he left behind all the dresses he'd made, the trunk full of petal skirts and wings, the tinsel trims, even the little pot of glittery cream he left for me to play with.

'Let Francie be the Christmas fairy from now on,' his letter said.

But I threw all the lovely things away.

The things he told her

This time of year the maidengrass was waist-high. Carolina stood at the big kitchen window looking out over it, the near paddock swathed in the fine greeny yellow grass that wavered and rippled in the breeze like hair. She could imagine how it would feel to be standing amongst it, the fine grass at her waist, around her legs. There would be the sweet scent of late summer, earth, a high sky, and everything around her rich and ripe and yellowgreen.

How far the season was in and yet it was still so warm outside. Already the ground was crumbled in parts for the first harvest, the stock animals heavy in the home pens – yet Carolina felt more at peace to be standing by the kitchen window than doing any other thing. Seeing to vegetables in the garden, washing dishes and putting them away in the tall cupboards, calling out to the boys, had they done their chores, would they come in for tea . . . She found herself sometimes in the midst of one of these small gestures, and a feeling of panic would come over her, a queer dark space opened up inside. She may be drawing a wet wash sponge across the bench, bending to the floor with a dustpan and brush and she would have to stop suddenly, clutch herself at her chest. She would turn, as if to balance herself, but the darkness was at the edge of her vision then, like something leaked, a blot, or a mark. A thin bleed across the clarity of her eye.

⋆

She never used to feel this way, separate from her husband and children, dreaming about stillness and quietness when there was so much to do. And all through the summer, Ray had been working on the farm just the same, and never suspecting that she could be standing doing nothing, in this house he'd made for her, with all this land around her, just standing in the middle of the kitchen or the bedroom, or at the window . . . He never knew. There were the children getting ready for a new school term and full of it, the coloured books for reading, their little boxes and containers for pencils she'd bought for them in town, and none of them had noticed that all the things they needed from her, would continue to need . . . She was finding more difficult to give them. It was as if all the rooms Carolina had to care for were too big and the land too big for Ray, pulling on his clothes in the morning and leaving while she was still half-asleep.

'Bye, baby.'

He would just put his hand on her shoulder, on her breast, just lean down in the dark to kiss her and the emptiness inside her would open up then, in the early morning light – all this land and space to work in and nothing they could do would make a difference. Her nightdress would not seem enough to cover her, and she would feel naked in the bed, available to him as though they were newly married. He would reach for her, and it was like being woken out of herself, the sudden tang of his skin against her skin, his ripe mouth against her mouth. He would reach for her in the dark and the panic was there, it fluttered like wings.

'Bye, baby.'

It was as if he wasn't her husband, the man she woke to, lay in the room with and listened to the sounds of him dressing. As if she didn't know him so well that she could guess the exact clothes he was picking up from the chair. The thick woollen socks she'd knitted for him last Christmas. The heavy work shirt he'd had since they'd been together, that had belonged to his father and was patched and darned like scribbling all over the check pattern, but he wouldn't wear anything else. She knew how the matted surface of the shirt kept rain out, and snow. She knew how he could ride in that shirt, if he was out for days at a time, handle livestock and get filthy in it but still he would always wear it the next day, summer, winter. She knew all these details as a wife would know the clothes of the man she had married, and it was something that had always come easy to her, to be attentive. To know how Ray liked meat to be cooked, how cold the beer. To keep the house tidy, the freezer full, the boys clean in the mornings and ready for school. In all their detail she knew these things because together they made up her life – her family, her husband – proof they would be together always, in all the detail of fibre and fastening and matted wool.

★

Carolina moved closer to the window; she shivered.

Yet there was this feeling of emptiness now, undoing the seam between them, a darkness come upon her in the midst of her life, like a shadow on the pale blondness of the land, a mark in her eye. Outside, though there was the high grass in combed pieces all the way up the hill, the sky tender and blue like a cloth you would wrap babies in, she could feel it, fear. That the family she loved and cared for were not enough . . . or worse. That the darkness had not come upon her, but was inside her from the beginning, and that it would devour her, that she would lose them all.

Two weeks later and the summer was gone. Without warning, it was suddenly winter, a freak snowstorm blown up from the south, while there were still leaves hanging off the trees, apples, plums to be picked, when there were still pink and yellow roses putting out new blooms. A day or two passed and no sign of a melt and the weather had settled in by then, a deep, hard frozen ground underfoot, snow thick on the tops of the hills, ice binding even the branches and trunks of the cherry trees that grew close to the house.

★

Bitter, the cold started in and held, the lawn and garden like concrete, the boys kept falling on it, hurting themselves. Carolina would be soaking off bandages from their knees, dampening down their grazed and bleeding hands with Dettol, and they would run straight outside to fall again. Even when she managed to dig the flower beds over, the trenches of earth piled up and frozen were treacherous for their games, like graves. She found herself always worrying about the boys. That they were going to be too cold, that they didn't have enough clothes on. That playing on the hard ground was dangerous, that their little bones would snap.

She started calling to them earlier and earlier in the evenings, 'Come inside!'

She would be standing there at the doorway shivering, waiting for them to come in, and they would be off with the horses somewhere, or in the shearing shed. Playing football out in one of the empty paddocks, or over the hill.

'Come in!'
'Come inside!'
She called and called.

'Come in!'
'Please come inside now!'

★

It was as though she'd never felt this close to them before, fretting about their safety, tending to the open wounds in their fine undamaged skin. It was as if the suddenness of the cold had made her remember how much they depended on her for their care, and she in turn had never wanted to hold them, and bathe them in warm water and kiss them and protect them like she wanted to when that cold season first began.

Ray wasn't around, that could have been part of it. He'd gone to look at some land at a neighbouring farm, and then got stranded there in the storm. It seemed like months that he'd been away. Then one morning when the weather had settled he telephoned in to say he was coming home, bringing some cows that were due for early calving. No one could have expected the weather when the bull was put to season, he said, but the cows should be alright if he could get them into the home barns that night.

'I won't be late,' he said. 'Tell the boys I'll come in and say goodnight.'

That night the fire was burning, the range was on. It was warm enough inside, as though Carolina was able to compensate for the weather, as though by now the feelings of darkness and cold were to do with the temperature outdoors, nothing more, nothing she need panic about within herself, or fear. That night the children had been bathed and were in bed straight after supper, the baby in his cot and the two boys tucked neatly into their beds, side by side, their pyjamas buttoned and their hair dark against the pillows.

Davey had his books from school and he was pretending to read from them to the others.
'And then the sheriff said, "Hey! I know, let's head off on the horses and stay the night in the hills . . ."'
Carolina smiled, cowboys and Indians.
'"We can set up camp, I'll round up the men . . ."'
It was always guns and horses and the wild west.

She went back into the kitchen and started to wash the dishes, the story coming in pieces to her from down the hall.
'We could just hang around and wait for those Indian jokers,' Davey was saying.
'And then let's just kill 'em.'
'Yeah!'
'Use their own bloody old arrows!'
'Yeah!'
'Yeah!'
She was enjoying herself, the sound of the boys' voices in the background, the kitchen warm and comfortable and well lit. She took her time rinsing the glasses in hot water, drying each knife and fork separately while the noises from the bedroom gradually became louder and louder. Finally she went in to quieten them down.

*

By then the book had been thrown aside and the two boys were playing cowboys from their beds. Alec was jumping up and down on his mattress, all his covers in a twisted heap, and Davey had put on half the outfit she'd given him for his last birthday, the hat, and the waistcoat with the fringe and the special pocket for a gun. He'd piled his pillows onto his bed and was sitting astride them as if he was riding a horse, and there was the baby up at the bars of his cot looking out at everything.

'Now what's all this.'

Carolina went around the room straightening the covers, tidying away the bows and arrows that were tangled in the sheets. 'Quietly. Back into bed, properly now.'
She smoothed the pillowcases, found the baby's cuddly toy at the foot of his cot and gave it back to him. As she was doing that, putting it under the quilt and tucking the baby in, she looked at her watch and it occurred to her how late it was for Ray, how she thought he'd be in by now.

The boys didn't ask about him. She kissed them all goodnight, she turned off the lights, but before she left the room she stood there in the doorway a minute, the baby asleep already, the other two in their beds with their eyes closed, Davey with his hat still on. She looked at the three of them, these children she and Ray had made, these sons, and she wanted to rush up to them and keep them, entirely for herself. She wanted to swallow them whole and take them back inside herself, if that's what it took to keep them safe. How she loved them, wanted to bury her face in them, so intensely happy with her life at that moment she could hardly bear it.

And then she went back out to the kitchen and there was Ray.

He'd only just got in from putting the cows up. He was standing in the middle of the kitchen under the bright overhead light and although there was cold from outside gathered around his body where he stood, he was sweating. Steam rose off the wool of his shirt and his long mackintosh that was plastered around his legs. He'd taken his gumboots off at the back door as usual but even so his socks were muddy, his breeches were muddy. There was mud on his sweater, his shirt. There was a wet dark smear down his cheeks, across his brow so that his eyes seemed pale and white and crazy-looking.

Carolina gasped, for a second, not knowing who he was.

'What's happened?'
She managed to say that.
'Is everything alright?'
She started to walk towards him.
'Are the cows – ?'
'No, nothing like that.'

*

Then she stopped.

Ray was taking his clothes off. Right there in the kitchen, he was stripping off piece after piece of dirty clothing. First the coat, then the work shirt, then the sweater, the stockbelt. A great pile of dirty clothes lay in the middle of the kitchen floor. Then he took off the thermal undershirt and still he was as filthy as though there had been no clothes on him at all. There was mud up his arms, across his chest, mud on his hands, on his stomach a great smear of mud. Mud everywhere, only it didn't look like mud, Carolina thought. It looked like blood.

She stepped back.

My God, she thought.
What have you done?

'I've had a day,' Ray was saying. 'I've had a hell of a day, I tell you, babe, this weather. The cows are fine now but it took all afternoon, they were five miles easy past the pine border. Something had broken the wire and they'd wandered for pasture. There's nothing growing up there, the weather's killed it.' He was still taking his clothes off as he spoke, pulling off his gaiters, his socks, and his voice seemed loud, as if he was still outside, in the midst of the wet and cold, out in some field or other, up on some hill in a hut, stripping off, telling some shepherd, or some other man or boy. 'So I brought them back the shorter way. Came down through the gully . . . Through the bloody bush . . .'

He reached down and picked the T-shirt off the floor, used it to rub the back of his neck, and his hair stiff and dark with mud. Carolina knew she should have gone towards him, to pick up the pile of clothes that were tumbled in a wet dirty heap on the floor, any other time she would have done it, stooped, bundled the dirty clothes together in her arms to throw into the washing machine. But again something stopped her. The idea of the bush, soaking wet and dark in the cold, the slick ground with its layers of decomposing foliage . . . The idea of the dark growth of the bushes and trees and how it must have been for one man on a horse, bringing pregnant cows through it, down one of those narrow muddied trails. No one to help him keep the animals moving, as the rain poured through the leaves, no one to help him control them, keep them in line.

'Ray, that's a crazy thing,' she said. 'You never should have done it, not in this weather, on your own. No wonder you're so late . . . I can't believe –'

'Listen,' he cut her short.

And there was something about the way he said that word.

'You'd better be careful. You. The boys.'

*

He started walking towards her in his underwear.

'I want you to really watch it from now on. I think there's a boar loose, in the bush close to the farm. Something. I can't think what else brought the fence down.'
He was walking towards her as he spoke, getting closer and closer. The T-shirt he had used to wipe his hair was balled like a rag in his hand, like it was wrapped around something, a gun, a stone.
'I want you to be careful,' he was saying. 'All the way, coming back down through the track, the cows were spooked, the horse was playing up. There's something there, and it's not that far away, either, giving hell. Near the track the bush was all broken up, something had trampled the small stuff away, there was just mud up there and I saw some tracks, Jesus, they were big enough. I mean it, be careful. A pig that size can go for a woman or a child if it's got a mind to. I knew a guy last year lost two of his dogs to a boar, took them into the bush to track it and the bloody thing turned on them. Took one dog straight off and maimed the other. Then, here's the thing, the next night it came back to finish what it had started. It dragged the injured dog clean out of its kennel, took it away off into the bush . . .'

He was right in front of her, looking at her with his pale, pale eyes.

*

'So you see, you've got to watch out,' he said. 'They can be dangerous animals. Tell the boys, they have to play near the house from now on.'

He was still looking at her, warning her. Carolina couldn't move.

Then he turned away and stepped out of his underpants.

Suddenly, at that minute with his back to her, under the bright light of the kitchen, Ray's shyness, his buttocks pale and vulnerable, was like a little boy's. After the dark face, after those awful words . . . Carolina felt her relief like a sigh, as if she could breathe again. There was still the filth of the rest of his body, the steaming mass of saturated clothes, but for a minute, just then, as he was turned shyly away, she wanted to rush up to him with the same feeling she'd had for the children earlier, that she would hold him, protect him from this awful thing he'd discovered. That she would keep her arms around him, around those ribs, that waist, those parts of his body that were white and scared-looking as a child's.

The light of the kitchen seemed to flood her, Carolina felt its warm yellow reflected off the Formica surfaces, off the linoleum floor. If she could just keep this man, she thought, look after him like she had been able to look after her children, fear for him as she had feared for them . . . If she could just allow her heart to accommodate the concerns of more than one soul, then perhaps it would not seem so frail.

But she was a wife to him, not a mother. He had no need of her protection, he had no fear. He was the one out with his horses every day, checking on the sheep that were scattered all over the high hills, he knew where every flock was sheltering. He was the one out feeding the cattle wintering on the eastern lowland, land she'd never even seen, birthing early calves in barns that would be dark and cold and full of earth and shit. She was a wife, she wasn't to protect him. He was the one with naked arms and she should have taken comfort from them. She could have had those arms around her if she'd let him, instead of pretending she could hold him, tell him everything would be okay.

'I'm taking a shower,' he said now, walking towards the door. 'What's for dinner?'
Then he stopped, turned around fully naked, and she saw the dark streaks running down his body.

Of course she couldn't help him. He would scorn it. He would use her help to take his clothes off, to pull her towards him. He would use it for pushing himself towards her, for taking her tongue into his mouth like food. He there for him when he came over to her, kissed his index finger and tapped it on the tip of her nose. He smiled at her.

'I'm starving . . .'

But she couldn't. She couldn't smile back, she couldn't close her eyes to be kissed. She could only think about what he'd said about being alone out there, and the things he'd seen.

'Be careful,' she said. 'Please . . .'

But he just leaned down towards her and his face was wet with dirt, and she could feel where the strong white parts of his body that were not dirty were pressed up against her.

'This animal . . .' she tried to say. 'Aren't you worried –'

'Okay, okay.' He let her go. 'Okay?'

'But aren't you worried . . .' She tried again. 'You said we should be careful.'

Carolina could hear her small foolish voice, going on and on, asking about the animal that was loose and where it was and how big, he was just smiling at her, his teeth white and the whites of his eyes bright against the smeary dark of his face.

'Isn't it awful?' she asked him, 'this situation we're in, isn't it frightening? Aren't you frightened?'

'I'm just starving,' he said, and he turned and went out the door.

'Watch it, though,' he called, as he was walking away, down the hall towards the bathroom. 'I mean what I said before, I don't like wild pigs. They can be cruel buggers. If it looks like it's going to give us any trouble, I'm going to go after it.'

He laughed then, a curious, hard laugh, and the next second Carolina heard him start to sing.

'Oh I like a bit of piggy for my supper,
Cut piggy up and have him for my tea.'
His voice faded as he shut the bathroom door, but she could still hear it, first that strange false laugh she'd never heard before, and now this song, this cruel little song that was supposed to be funny but wasn't funny at all.
'Tell piggy when you meet him,
I've got a lovely knife.'

And she hated the new voice.

He had both taps on in the shower steaming hot, and he was singing.
'Oh piggy, piggy, piggy,
I'll have your lovely life.'

Carolina pulled her cardigan around her. She hated the song more than any other song she'd ever heard him sing. Drunk or sober, it was a horrible, frightening little song.

She told the boys the next day, at breakfast, just like Ray had said. They were to be careful, they must play close to the house, but even as she heard her words she knew how the story was only an adventure to them, the most exciting kind of game.
Davey said, 'Are you sure it's big and mean, Mum? The pig?

Is it a pig that's bigger than you? Is the pig bigger than Dad, even? Does it have those big bones coming out of its head . . .'
Both he and Alec were sitting at the kitchen table, their bowls of cornflakes in front of them uneaten.
'Not bones . . .' she said.
Even the baby had his head on one side, as if he was listening, wanting to know every detail of how dangerous the animal could be. All of them, all three of them, their father's sons.
'I'm serious about this,' she said. 'And they're not bones, they are tusks, and they can hurt you. I mean it, Davey. No taking Alec and the baby further than the home paddock, no playing in the sheds. Dad says the boar can come too near a farm in winter when it gets hungry.'
Davey smiled at that.
'Will it come looking for us, Mum? To start gobbling us up?'
He was holding his spoon up like a little spear, his face flushed with excitement, and Alec just sat, his eyes wide, his mouth open, listening to every word his brother was saying.
'I mean it,' Carolina said. 'You must be very very careful . . .'
'Wow!'
Now Davey rushed at his cornflakes, cramming spoonfuls into his mouth.
'Like this, Alec,' he said, spooning them in, and the younger boy started doing the same.
'Like this, Mum,' he joined in, and he was gobbling up his cornflakes as fast as he could, always wanting to copy his older brother, be as brave and as clever and as loud.

'I'm a big boary pig and I'm eating you up! Yah!'
Davey stuck his spoon out at the baby.
'Yah!' shouted Alec. 'Me too!'
'I'm eating you up!'
The baby started to cry.
'Stop it!'
Carolina snatched away both boys' spoons.
'Don't make fun. It's serious. You must promise me. You must be careful, I don't want you going near the bush. Play close to the house now, you promise me!'

Weeks passed after that night when Ray came home, and the dark empty feeling she'd had over summer was deep within her now, and the danger had its own form and shape. She could not shake free of the thought of the wet cold of the bush and the size of the animal in it, plundering through the trees and plants and muddy ravines, wet stripping off its back, the plume of its breath. She could imagine what it looked like, as though the sight of it had been her own possession. The long blunted tusks, the tooth protruding from the lower jaw. She felt she could smell the animal, its hot breath, its thick piss on the rotting leaves, the rank meaty sweat of its hide. She could sense it, close by, grunting as it came out into a clearing, panting, the way it would peer about the dense undergrowth, trying to see the way forward with its tiny pig eyes.

*

During the day she found herself thinking more and more about everything that had happened that first night, Ray coming in from the cold and the things he told her. She would remember the sight of him as he came into the kitchen to tell her there was an animal loose in the bush. She would think about the way his face had been smeared and splattered with mud, how she'd thought it was blood. She remembered his grin, the way he'd rolled his pale eyes at her as a joke and how he'd started to sing that song, the way he'd laughed when he joked about killing the boar and eating it. Again and again she heard the sound of Ray's strange laugh as he'd walked down the hall towards the shower.

'They can be crazy old buggers,' he'd said to her, later that same night, when she was getting undressed for bed. 'Crazy, you know? *Loco*. Those tusks, they can kill you, baby, with one touch. Better cuddle up close and don't let him come too near.' He'd reached out and gripped her, it was supposed to be a game, and then he'd snuffled into her back when they were lying together under the covers. He'd seemed excited by the whole idea, taking up a handful of her nightdress and pulling it as if he would tear it off her.

'Grunt, grunt,' he'd said. 'There's something coming, baby. I can feel it in the dark.'

She'd panicked, 'Don't!', but still he'd come at her, he'd wrapped his arms around her. He could do anything with those arms, she'd seen him pull back a bull's head to slit its throat with those arms, sling sheep up over his shoulder. Now this. He would go after some animal in the bush using those same arms, like he would go after her.

'Grunt, grunt.'

Using his body on her like a weapon. He'd go after this animal alone, in the bush, in the dark.

'Grunt, grunt.'

'Please don't!'

She'd pulled away.

'I mean it, Ray!'

'Okay, okay.'

He'd shifted, turned over.

'Take it easy.'

She'd hurt his feelings she knew, but then he'd gone to sleep straight away, as if nothing had passed between them at all, and she'd lain awake for hours, feeling the darkness outside as though it were in the room with her, something she was breathing.

From that night on Carolina found it harder and harder to be near Ray in the bed. The minute he was asleep she'd get up, start moving around the house, looking for something, warmth or rest, but she couldn't find either. She started going over to stand by the window in the kitchen, a little heat still coming from the stove for comfort, she would look through the black glass at the garden and the paddock, everything black and cold out there, but gradually her eyes made out the difference, the paler black of the grass and the dark black strip that was the beginning of the bush. There in the distance she could see it, the dark strip, the ridge of black that started there in the gully and went back right across the hill behind, and the hills behind that, covering all the hills all the way to the mountains beyond. The image of this dark growth, this thick fertile mass of foliage and undergrowth . . . All winter the image itself seemed to grow on Carolina like tendrils and choking vines.

Ray seemed to forget all about what he'd said, about the boar, about how they'd all have to be careful they didn't go out far from the house. There was so much else to do. The cold had caused him to lose a lot of sheep and he'd had to burn the carcasses up on the hills, riding way off to the edge of the farm, and camping there with one of the shepherds. Together they would spend days in the snow, turning the heavy Perendales that had toppled onto their backs with the weight of wool, baling out extra feed, getting the early lambing ewes into sheltered pens. Even when he wasn't staying away from the house, Carolina didn't see much of him. He'd leave early in the mornings, leaning in to kiss her in the dark, goodbye, the smell and press of him like sex from the night before. It was too much, his heavy body, the weight of it upon her, his arms encircling her body and keeping it, like something live caught in roots, trunks. He would lean into her and she would allow her cheek towards him but his greedy mouth always wanted her mouth.

*

Grunt, grunt.

That's what the children would have said too, just like their father, pretending to be little pigs with little pigs' greedy, hungry mouths.

Grunt, grunt.

Her own husband an animal in the bed.

Only after he'd left in the mornings could she feel relaxed, feel her limbs free of his weight. Nothing had happened. She had been safe, the boys were safe. There had been no harm come to the farm, the animals . . . Yet still, Carolina felt afraid, the dark still seemed to come too early. Ray may have forgotten what he said but she couldn't forget, and every day it seemed like the bush was getting closer, closer to the house. As the dark came in, there were noises, she thought she heard them coming from outside.

By late winter Ray may as well never have told her about the boar, it was as though he had never in his life seen traces of that creature. He'd long since fixed the fence that had been trampled through, and with all the breeding cows in the near paddocks he had no requirement to bring others down the bush track as he'd done all those months ago. Every now and then Carolina mentioned it to Ray, had he seen anything when he'd been out on the hill, or if he'd cut into the bush at all on his way home some days, had he seen any marks, tracks. She would ask him, 'You know that pig you thought there might be in the bush . . .' And he wouldn't look up at her, to answer. He would just keep eating or watching the news programme, and after a while he might say, 'Yeah? What was that?', and if she said it again, he would just say, 'Oh, that thing. Don't worry about that thing,' as though he'd never talked about it in the first place. As if he'd never come in late that night dirty, and bringing with him his sex and his fear.

It was so quiet during the day. With both boys at school, she just had the baby at home. He slept or he watched her from his playpen. She would put him down and he would sleep through the morning, through the afternoon. He was so quiet. Not like the other two when they were little. Sometimes Carolina forgot he was even there, she would forget to look in on him, or when he was up she wouldn't notice him, but then would turn and see him in his corner, his eyes on her. She remembered how he'd screamed that morning when Davey made the pig noises. It seemed so long ago. She couldn't think he'd made a noise since.

Hours passed in this silence, brief spasms of sunlight caught in the glass of the windows and trapped the heat but Carolina never opened them, she never went outside. She heard the clock tick in her warm rooms, the house seemed huge. Then perceptibly the days became longer, green came back to the fields and trees. The hens started roosting again. Still there was this darkness at the corner of her eye, still this standing around for hours, watching the colours change in the day, from morning to lunch to afternoon, but Carolina felt she should have got better, with the growth of the new season, with the maidengrass starting to come back to the fields outside again. She began to think that the conditions of her heart should give her ease.

The lambing started and Ray was up even earlier in the mornings, out the whole day and bringing back the stray orphans where the ewes had died in birth. Pretty soon the back kitchen was filled with lambs bedded down and the sound of them bleating for milk. It kept Carolina busy, all the little hungry mouths. It reminded her, preparing bottles, Ray taking a lamb out of her arms into his own, of her marriage.

Towards the end of spring, all the lambs were big enough to go outside. There was a sense of something achieved, a sense of having overcome the difficulties of feeding and care to make a new life strong. One evening, when she and Ray were putting out the last six of the lambs, before supper, the two of them together out there in the yard, she found herself reaching for her husband. She put her arms around him and started to hug him, she took him to her. Closer, she held him, and closer, for so long he'd seemed far away and now she couldn't have him close enough.

He pulled back at first, surprised. Then he grinned at her. 'Well this makes a change,' and he put his hands in her hands. 'I thought it was something I'd done.'
'C'mon.'
She pressed against him.
'What,' he said. 'Now?'
He looked around. The boys were playing with the new lambs, they would be busy that way for an hour or so at least.
'Well, okay.'
And she pulled him inside. Suddenly, ravenous, and light, like all the blackness of the earlier months had been a dream and she was young and in love again with this tall strange man she would undress for, be kissed and touched by . . . The one she would let herself be all movement for, to wind around him in circles, this strange strong man in the bed.
'Well, hey.'
And she said, 'Now', and everything had been fine between them. It had been fine.

It could have stayed that way, she really felt it should have stayed. All the things he'd said before, and all the things he'd done that she'd so feared, and all the things he hadn't said, that could have helped, and the things he hadn't done . . . All these things that had made her scared for so long seemed to fade then, vanish into sweat and kisses. All of it . . . was gone. She lay in the sheets afterwards, cool and dissolved, and outside she could hear the boys playing and the gentle sounds of spring, the birds, the little cat on the window sill opening its mouth to mew, waiting for her kittens to be born.

Then, in the midst of such gentleness, Ray kissing her gently, half-asleep, an awful sound pierced through the sky. Then there was screaming, Davey screaming.

'What the –'

In a flash Ray was out of bed, he pulled on his jeans and ran outside. Carolina couldn't do anything at first, she lay shock still, everything in her frozen by the awful sound of that cry. Then she jumped up, flung her dress over her head and followed him.

The boys were standing in the middle of the paddock as before, Alec had the baby's hand in his. It was just as before, when Carolina had last seen them except now there were no lambs around them in the enclosure, they were scattered. There was a large gash in the fence and blood trails. Then there was a crash in the undergrowth beyond the paddock, something dark. Carolina gasped. Couldn't breathe.

There was something.

There was something.

*

'What are you doing, for godsake?'

Ray had turned on her, was yelling at her, she couldn't hear any of the words. His face was full of hate and there were his pale, pale eyes.

Something.
Something.

She looked at him, not knowing him, and gradually the words he was yelling formed sentences in her mind.
'Go to the boys, for godsake,' the words were saying. 'Can't you see they're terrified straight out of their wits? Go to them! I'm getting my gun. Get the children, for godsake. Pull yourself together!'

She realized then, it wasn't that she hadn't been breathing. It had been screaming that had clenched her throat shut. Her own screaming stopping her breath. She saw Davey standing there looking at her in terror.
'It's alright, you know, Mum.'
He looked like he was about to cry. His face was pale, as if someone had taken a cloth and wiped all the expression from it.
'It's alright, Mum. It didn't gobble us.'
The baby was crying, Alec was crying.

'It's alright,' Davey was saying. 'It was going to eat that little lamb, it was my lamb. It had bones, Mum, and the lamb was caught on the bones . . .'

Carolina put out her hand to touch him, there, she put her hand on his head, the soft feathers of his hair. This tiny little boy and all the words he'd said, not crying, trying not to cry. 'I know, darling,' she said. 'Come inside. Come inside, boys.' She was able to say that, thank God she was able to say that, to take them by the hand and walk with them towards the door.

Then Ray came running out of the house.
'I told you to get inside!'
His face was full of hate.
'Now!'

He didn't shoot the boar that night, or any night that week. The thing went on and on. Ray fixed up the patch in the fence but it came back, it got another lamb, and another. Ray sat up all night for seven nights, with the rifle loaded, waiting, ready for it as it came into the enclosure, when he could get it clean in his gun's sight. But after the third lamb had been taken, and during the day this time, he decided to take the stallion and go into the bush himself to track the animal down, and bring it back shot and dead. It was the only way.

⋆

Carolina helped him pack his rucksack but by then she and Ray could barely speak. All his thoughts were of bringing this thing back killed, and no more destruction to the farm, and Carolina couldn't tell him, Be careful, I love you. She couldn't tell him. It had been a long time since she had been able to feel like a wife, she saw how long it had been now that he may need her to be with him and she had forgotten how.

Early the next morning Ray left on horseback with his gun. She waited.

It took three days and nights before he came back. She heard the horse first, looked out the window and saw the horse and Ray leading it, and something heavy across the horse's back, half hanging down onto the ground, something. She stood, she couldn't go out to the door. She saw them come through the paddock, the man and the horse and the thing dragging on the ground.

She pulled her cardigan close. She was cold. Now she was always cold. She shivered, a huge shiver that ran the length of her body, contorted her face. What had happened to her that she had become so twisted? Where was the tender sky? The maidengrass that had grown so long and she could stand amongst it like a girl? Still she couldn't move from where she was standing. The thing was coming closer. She pressed her fingers to her lips as though she was going to scream or be sick and she had to stop herself.

Ray stepped in the door.

Not mud on him this time, blood. Black blood like oil on his face, down his arms. He smiled at her and it should have been a relief to see the blood, should have been.

'Done!' he said. He walked towards her. 'He's a big boy, too. Come out and see him, sweetheart.' Ray put out his hand, to take her hand, and his hand was black with the blood of the thing he'd killed. There was blood in him so deep it was etched into his skin like dye. There was blood under his fingernails.

'No!'

Carolina could see it out there now, huge. With its gaping dead mouth open and its body laid across the horse's back and full of that same blood.

'No! No!'

And she started shaking her head from side to side.

'No, no, no.'

Whimpering, not crying, just making these little sounds to herself, these small frightened noises coming from her that she'd never heard before, never knew she had inside her before.

'No, no, no . . .'

Like a tiny animal.
Like something that was barely alive.

'Hey,' Ray came closer, close enough to touch her. Like she was an animal he might scare with touch, like she was an animal he could trap or kill.
'Baby.'
His eyes were pale.
'Baby.'
Slowly his hand came out to touch her hand.
'No!'
Carolina screamed, a ribbon of sound from her throat.
'No! You!'
She ran from him.
'No, never you!'
She was screaming and screaming. Running.
'Get away from me! Take your thing away from me! I don't want to see it! Don't make me see it!'

How she had hurt him.

How she had pushed him away when he came home and needed comfort . . .

How she had run.

★

How she had made their bedroom a room where only she could stay.

Later, much later, when it was dark, she was standing in the corner of her room and Ray came to the door, but she didn't answer.
'It's nothing,' he was saying through the door. 'What's happened, honey? What's the matter? Let me help you. Let me in, open the door, don't turn me away.'

It was hours ago. Days ago. Nights ago.

How she had hurt him then.

Now she stood in the big kitchen window. She stayed there, in that place where she had been before, where it was home. This glass. This piece of linoleum under her feet, home. And the grass was there, beyond the window, like before, and the day outside was high and fine like it was before.

She could see the grass.

It had grown so tall, it would be so soft upon her.

⋆

She thought how she could go out into the grass, there in the depths of the yellowgreen of the grass and no one would ever find her when she walked amongst it. Ray would never find her, the boys would never find her. There would be just the maidengrass, the soft grass everywhere they looked, the maidengrass and she herself a maid within it, a maid herself that she could come so undone from wife and mother, that she could walk out into the green and gold and never return, that she could leave them all behind. There would be no more screaming, or words. No more heavy limbs leaning on her limbs, no more sounds in the night and words for killing, no animals that came in the night, opened their red mouths wide and picked up her little boys, and took the man who was her husband, and carried them all away.

Only the grass, only the greeny gold and no blood.

She could leave. The animal. The red mouth. All the strength of the men here on this land she could leave. Their words, their knives for birthing and killing, even the little picture-books for the babies full of killing, she could leave. Gather up her skirts, a maid herself in the grass.

Only the grass to take her.

Then Carolina heard something quiet, something so quiet and soft. Behind her, where she stood at the window, at the glass.

*

She was not alone.

They were there. Somewhere in the house she had been given, or on the land that she still loved. Somewhere. Husband. Children. Somewhere, in one of her warm rooms, in a part of her planted garden. They were there as though they were gathered around her, those who she could leave, she dreamed of leaving, who she could never leave. How leave, those cries in the dark who were her? Those heavy arms? The eyes that she kissed closed. How ever leave? The children splayed in bed sleeping and the light still on? Their small bodies, small wounds that needed her bandaging? How ever leave them, the little children, when they were her?

She turned from the window, from the glass. She turned.

Whatever came for her she could only protect them, there was no other thing for her to do. Even from herself she would protect them. From the red mouth, protect. Let her own body be taken whole into it, so those she loved could run away from the beast.

Only protect them, there is nothing else to do.

Only let the darkness inside her that she fears also be the

darkness of infinite gentleness, the mouth for killing the same mouth that carries the babies safely away.

Only take care.

Be watchful over them.
This man, these children.
Let them be safe.
Only let their own mouths be wide open, laughing into the air, under that tender sky.

This place you return to is home

For M.G. and M.G. – in memory

I remember these certain days when everything was bright. The little white and red and yellow flowers in the grass, they were bright, and the grass, bright like green needles coming up in shoots but it never seemed to hurt us. We used to run across it, across the flowers, and nothing cut because our feet were tough. I remember Laura and I touching the soles of each other's feet, the grey dark skin, dirty from running on tar and stones and earth, we would touch each other there and we would never feel it, the lightness of our fingertips drawing patterns upon our skin.

'I can't feel you.'

There, the voice of my sister.

'You could cut me, and I wouldn't feel. You could pinch me hard.'

It was a game we played, something for toughness. And we thought we could be like boys, not sisters, like twins, we could be like little clever boys because we did things the same, in every way the same. Running out onto the lawn together, to spin together on the grass, turning round and around and around. It had to be that way.

'Look at me!'

*

There again, the voice of my little sister.

And I would call out too, as I turned on the green needles.

'See me too! I'm playing too!'

That was how the days went, the bright days when nothing could touch us or cut or mark. We played for everybody. For our parents, the teachers at school. We played for the doctors who spied on us, for the sly children who watched Laura and whispered about her behind her back. Everybody.

Except our grandmother. She alone understood that smallest child with the twisty limbs, with her funny sentences, with her pixie smile. Laura and I could play and play together, but our grandmother alone knew how it was a game.

We used to call out to her from the lawn, 'Play with us, Nani!' and sometimes she would come and sit with us, let us tickle her under her dress, let Laura touch her eyelids when she closed her eyes. She would seem to be asleep for a moment –

'Can you feel this?'
And Laura would be touching her, lightly, lightly all over her face, smoothing her face and her hair, patting and touching her closed eyes.

'And this?'
Then our grandmother would open her eyes.
'My darling girl,' she said.
And she would gather Laura in.
'I didn't feel a thing.'

My sister could have been that woman's very own child, people used to say, they used to murmur amongst themselves about amounts of love that could be given. It was true, my grandmother loved my sister more, but she looked after us both, cared for us both during those long summer holidays away from our parents. We could stay for weeks, months, and no one else was there. Nobody to come up close to us and ask questions. Nobody we needed to dress for in certain ways, or reply 'It happened this way, sir.' We could play any games we wanted but with our grandmother we never had to pretend.

My sister didn't have to pretend.

She could do anything she liked there. She could whisk up her skirt, like she loved to do, she could spin on the lawn, singing and shouting out loud into the air –
'I got no knickers on!'
She could run and run, faster and faster, her hair flying out, her skirt flying out around her –

'I ain't got them on!
'I ain't got them on!'

She could take all her clothes off, if she wanted, she could bury her shoes in a pile of earth. She could call out late in the night, tell magic stories and sometimes laugh and cry. She could turn her food from her plate clean onto the floor . . . And our grandmother just said, 'Come here, darling,' and even though Laura was nearly nine she would crawl up onto Nani's lap like she was a little girl. She would let her head back, her hair fall back softly for stroking.

And our grandmother would whisper to her, 'Shhh, quietly.' And she would stroke and comb with her fingers the soft hair falling down.
And everything became quiet then as if all the children in the world were quiet, and all the birds and animals.
'Shhh, darling.
'Let's just be gentle and quiet, you and I.'

~

How I indulge that memory of quietness now, to bring myself comfort. How I let myself return. The time spent at our grandmother's house, weeks of time, but it seems like our lives were there.

★

It was a very old house. In the sense of untended, old. Old, too, in years, but for a child ancient, the way the white paint had peeled from the boards, the roof on the verandah sagged to let rain in, allowed swallows to nest in the corners and they were rarely startled. The weathering on the house, to me now beautiful enough but to a child a gorgeous thing, the bare bones of a house let out for anyone to see, foundation, underboard. And beautiful, the lines of that carelessness set against the order of colour and shape, the pattern of tall blooms and deep clustered borders, our grandmother's garden.

She used to say 'A wreck of a house!' – can anyone imagine something more thrilling to a child? A house that was totally careless! That sat, amidst lawns and flower beds, the many windows in summer propped open with kindling, the front door not quite shutting on its last hinge – can anyone imagine? The joy of running through rooms that were simply left to sit, unbrushed, unpolished. Left with strange pairs of shoes in them, beds with thin mattresses but no sheets, no pillows or covers. How I remember the empty, quiet pleasure of those rooms, with sunlight streaming through the windows, the carpets worn so close to the floorboards they were like silks, threads. In her sitting room a fire burned most days, and in the kitchen, it didn't matter that it was summer. The radio played. We drank black tea with honey, as much treacle sugar on our porridge as we wanted. And all the rooms sat around us at our back, silent and filled with sun.

'A wreck of a house', but no.

Beautiful white bones in your garden.
Beautiful windows always open wide to let in the sun.

Though I know my grandmother often found fault with the place, a floorboard that needed fixing, a skirting board broken from the wall and now mice could get in there, though I heard her talk about bleached curtains and damp in the winter, how even the tin that kept flour had a rusty lid that was too big . . . Still, in the kitchen, when she dusted the table with flour from that same tin, when she let us leave crumbs for the mice from the scones she'd made, and cake – she knew. Beneath the complaints about broken boards and threadbare coverings, she tended the carelessness, let the swallows stay. She allowed the bones to show: the emptiness to fill the space like prayers fill churches, the dusty, sunny air like incense inside her home.

Do you remember?

Outside, in our grandmother's garden, the roses climbed the trellis like their faded sisters in our room.

⋆

Close your eyes. Can you see?

There was wallpaper in our bedroom, the only part of the house to have it, a lovely pattern of pale pink and yellow blooms. Beyond our window, the real flowers were deeply-coloured damask rose and a yellow like Cornish butter, while next to them, in borders, were poppies and cornflowers and massed beds of stocks, fronds of wild scented dill.

Do you remember? The garden and the flowers?

How the roses had been so trained that their heads peeped into our window and the scent of their petals filled all those pale lemon and grey rooms? Do you remember you used to breathe in that lovely fragrance; you closed your eyes.

Bowls of roses stood in the circles of lamplight and at night, these gorgeously-grown, these pruned and trained blooms were made even more beautiful, the stems held all the more straight, the petals gathered around their centres in even more perfect silken knots, because the furniture around them was shaky and half broken, because the curtains hung without linings down the wall. Our grandmother made it that way, I know that now, the outside made safe by her garden, the outline of trellis and border and hedge. Did it matter that a door didn't lock between outside and in, that a twig held open the glass? There was no one to keep out.

Nothing beyond the garden, beyond the roses and their circles of light.

Do you remember? How we were safe there?

Now you're in this dark room with only a small yellow light by your bed . . .

Can I make for you in words that safe place where we can stay?

In the city, at our parents' house, the light was so different, white light. At our grandmother's, the sun came slowly into our bedroom, onto the faded flowers papered on the walls, through the curtains that were thin like clouds. It woke us slowly. The trees in the paddock beyond the garden used to wave to us, good morning, and all their little leaves and branches were warm and full of air. In town, it could never be the same. Our parents had built a house of rock and steel and plates of frosted glass that made the light white in all the rooms, on all the surfaces and doors. The floors echoed, there were no enclosures. Day and night, I would hear my parents move about through the structure of their home, listening through the white walls for sounds they didn't want to hear.

'What's going on in there?'
'Nothing!'

They would walk about, talking quietly to each other, then stop, call again through their partitions, through their frosted glass doors.
'Are you sure you're alright in there?'
'Is everything okay?'
'Everything's fine,' I used to call back to them. 'We're fine in here.'
Of course we had to say everything was fine. There was no one else there to say it. Even on the mornings when Laura woke frightened, when she would be sitting straight up in bed as if sleep had only been for a second, and the queer white light would be blaring all around her . . . Still, we had to make it into a game that nothing was wrong.

Those mornings she'd sit straight up and start talking and singing.
'I'm sorry, I'm sorry, I'm sorry.'
Her voice getting louder and louder.
'Shhh, darling.'
Her mouth getting wider and wider, calling out words, songs.
'I am . . . sorry . . .'

And her head would start to sway, and by then it had truly started, like drums beating.

*

'I –'

'I –'

My tiny little sister, this tiny child, turning, turning in the bed. Heaving her body from side to side, making it huge, making her mouth huge for words but only sounds coming out.

'I –'

'What's happening in there?'
'Nothing! We're fine!'

And quickly I would get out of my bed and run to where her body was twisting, and I would call out loudly with my own voice, so our parents couldn't hear her voice, so no one would hear her voice –
'It's a game! I know the game! You're not the only one who can play it!'
Even while she was making this sound, as if she was trying to speak, with some huge words deep in her throat –
'I –'
– my voice could be louder than hers:
'You're not the only one! You're not the only one!'
Even while her hair would be stuck up in pieces like wings,

like glass, like she was flying, we could make it into a game, the thin blood scratched down her arms, a game, the glass light in the room, all the sounds in the room a game, my voice calling out loudly the same as hers –

'It's a game, you know. I can play it! You're not the only one!'

'I –'

'What's happening in there?'

'Nothing!'

– they were only words she was trying to say!

'I –'

Not choking or gasping, not trying to bring some huge thing up out of her, a dark thing, some people would murmur . . .

'I –'

Only words!

'I –'

'What's going on in there?'

'Nothing's going on in here!'

Please stop worrying, I wanted to say. I want to say it now.

Be still.

Be gentle.

'I –'

★

Everybody, be gentle.
Step back.
Don't grab her shoulders like that, don't hold her like that.
'I –'
Even now, they are only words she's trying to say.

And they come out of her like sighing, like crying. 'I'm sorry! I'm sorry!' And there's her poor naked skin, turning, turning in the bed, still turning like it used to turn those mornings long ago, the way her body pulled her then, backwards and forwards, her fingernails running down her arms, down her soft sides.

'Don't,' I say, but not wanting to say it.
Only wanting to say, It's fine, everything's fine.

And like those mornings I would take her arms and I would be saying, 'It's a game, it's only a game.'
So I take her arms now.
Making my voice the same as hers, my words the same as hers.
'I'm sorry too. I'm sorry too.'
And like those mornings, while I was singing and rocking with her on the bed, the light would slowly go out, and I smoothed my sister's hair. So now, slowly, slowly. I let go of one of her arms, then the other arm.
'Still a game, only quietly, quietly the game.'

And slowly it works, my rocking with her on the bed, even more slowly, slowly, quietly.

'Shhh . . .'

Remember?
Her stroking your soft hair?

And I can stroke your hair now, tell you, 'Quietly, quietly.'
Just like she used to do.
'And nothing strange about Laura, see.
'It was only a game. Everything is fine here.'
And she has slowed now, almost to stillness, her arms moving just slightly up and down, like calmness, gentleness.
'Shhh . . .'

Just like our grandmother used to do.

Hard to believe now that the thin walls of her home could contain us when hot winds blew at the partly opened windows that never sat properly in their frames, and at the door that moved day and night on its frail hinge. Hard to believe that one woman, herself a house, could in the circle of her arms so contain us. Here she was, in her kitchen toasting bread for breakfast, or stirring cups of sweetened tea, and she could form a pattern for our lives, as sure as a design made in spilled sugar on her tablecloth, the outlines of a life. A radio voice in the background. The ordered sound of washed and dried dishes being put away.

'I can always look after you girls, you know,' she said to me, and she showed me how to use the telephone to make long-distance calls, so even when we were away from her we could still imagine that her circle was around us.

'Whenever you need to, you know how to telephone me. Just ring my number and I can come and get you, or I can make sure Mummy will put you on a train straight to me here.'

And so I would call, when my mother wasn't listening, or when she was in with Laura, or the doctor was there, Laura crying, not able to stop crying, and my father was rushed home from work – I went to the telephone then, I called the operator. I would give the operator my grandmother's number, so far away it would seem to me, with the noise at my back and the unyielding structure of my parents' home around me, their corridors and their glass. To hear the telephone ringing in my grandmother's house, far away, to hear her pick up the phone –

'Yes? Hello?'

. . .

Quietness again.
The circle drawn.

Hard to believe, yet didn't we manage it for a time? I look back and see her, this elderly woman, powerless in the world against the rest, and yet she would be on the phone to our parents the next morning, and their faces would be pale with lack of sleep, their little mouths outlines, and one or other of them would say, 'Your grandmother thinks you should go to her house for a few days, you and your sister. A few days, maybe a week or two, but what do you think of that for an idea? Would you like to?'

And of course after the night before, the sounds they couldn't bear to hear – of course it was what everybody wanted.

My mother, with her poor thin smile.
'Would you like to?'
She wanted it most of all.

How was it that she could have come from that other woman, come out of that other strong quiet body to run around and worry and cry out to our father in the night, 'Help me! I don't know what to do!'

What made her worry and worry, when for my grandmother, my sister was only a joy, a gift we could have for a time, to look after, a delicate thing we wanted to be careful with, to see that she would not break?

My mother wore glasses. She took them off, put them on, took them off again, when she spoke to me. She wanted me to understand. How vulnerable she was, her fears, all the things that she needed.

'You see, Beth, I worry too much about your sister. Look at my hands,' and she put out her thin white hands, her fingers stretched out like bones. 'They're shaking.'

But how could it be? My mother wrapped herself so tightly in the clothes she wore, surely she could not tremble? Her tight skirts and jackets that belted at the waist or buttoned through, her shoes strapped hard onto her feet, her tightly-closed bag filled with books as she clutched it. When you reached for her, it was the fittings of her, the buttons and seams, the thick double weft of fabric and lining and underskirt that you felt, stitched cloth and lining. How could she, so fitted, have come out of that other body that barely allowed clothes at all? How could my mother's tweeds and gaberdines be fashioned from someone who hardly ever wore a cardigan, who never wore anything with buttons or closings if she could help it?

My mother, who was a professor of English, used the word

'savage'. 'It's not nice, you know,' she used to say to me, when Laura and I returned from our holidays with our blackened toughened feet. 'It's not polite, only savage, the way your grandmother lives, denying where she fits in with the world. You know that, don't you? That she lets you and your sister run wild as a kind of cruelty? You don't believe people really want to behave that way? As if no one else in the world exists? You can imagine, can't you, how, when I was your age, growing up with her, how hard it used to be for me?'

But, no, mother. You were the one more cruelly bounded by your own decisions, your own opinions. All those years you struggled to make a life you could be proud of, away from the tattered house. There was your brilliant mind always at work, reading, writing your papers, the lectures that you gave, and how hard for you to have this second daughter who tried the clever thoughts, who tested with her difference all the smooth paths of your logic. Cruel for you, mother, I can see that now, to have so twisted away that second beautiful damaged child from your sight.

And now I look back and see my sister spin for the final time.

*

She turns in a whirl on the grass, her yellow and white dress spinning out around her like a daisy, like a top. Like a sun. She's calling out into the open air, as if she might be screaming but that's only a word other people would say. She's not screaming. She's so happy here.

And I get up, from where I've been lying, in our grandmother's garden, everything is too bright, glittering brightness. Too bright to play. Still, I get up onto the grass that has sharpened itself on the bright air, onto the hard little flowers that are like enamels and brooches and pins, and spin with my sister too, round and around and around.

'See me too!' I call out with her, louder and louder, as if to my mother all those miles away, to my father, to the teachers, to the doctors in the long wards where they're going to keep Laura, out of the sun.

'It's a game, you know! I can do this too!'
I cry out. I cry out, like Laura, then I sing it, I make it a song, with a note, a tune. A game, make everything into a game, so my sister and I can be twins, like boys, like clever little boys.
'See me too!'
But the words fly out into the bright air and they come back empty, with no sound at all.
'See me too!'

*

Empty. Just a room, a bed.
'See me too!'
And you may move your head on the pillow, but there are no more games now. Only time.

Time finally, allowed to change things. In the end it's always time. I may be sitting with you here, by your sleeping bed, reading to you, but even as I try to make this story for you, I should know by now that time would take the words from my mouth, from the page, would change them:
Jewels everywhere in Nani's garden, no longer flowers.
Grass that stitched the earth together like needles, invisible threads pulling tight, deep into the ground.

'I won't ever leave you,' I used to say to my sister, but it was time, more than people, that had pulled together those parts that did not belong, and had cut clean away that most soft part so dearly wanted.

'I won't ever leave you,' I used to say, but I was getting older and she was still a tiny child.

I'd heard my parents and their frightened voices in the hall.
'We can't manage any longer on our own.'
Nothing could stop it.

*

Not a grandmother, not a house.
None of my words can stop it.

There was my mother taking her glasses off to polish them, polish them on the hem of her skirt.
'It's got to be now,' I heard her say to my father, and he was standing very still, holding himself very still, 'I know, I know,' and my mother was polishing – was she weeping? – with her little spectacles brittle in her hands.
'It must be now!'

No quietness there.
Only crying and the brittle glass.
No gentle quietness, darling, and climb onto Nani's lap.

Only turning, that last summer.

'Play with us, Nani!' we called out together in our game, as I want to call out now, for comfort, my comfort, to stop the words that brought you here, to this dark room, I want to call out now, 'Play with us, Nani!'

But Nani was inside. The phone call already come down the line – 'We've decided.'
'They're going to send my darling child,' she said, 'my only love, away.'